PORCELAIN

Published by Clockwork Dragon Books
www.clockworkdragon.net

First printing, July 2018
Second printing, January 2019

Porcelain is a work of fiction. People, places, and incidents are either products of the author's mind or used fictitiously. No endorsement of any kind should be inferred by existing locations or organizations within it.

No teenagers, spaceships, Marines, or aliens were harmed in the making of this book.

ISBN: 978-1-944334-29-1

HARPER REVOLUTION #1

PORCELAIN

LEE FRENCH

CHAPTER 1

Strawberry sauce is my nemesis. Every time I'm presented with a dessert including that sticky red delight, it's a challenge to avoid devouring the whole thing in ten seconds. Today, I faced my opponent in a battle of wills over cheesecake. I couldn't tell who was winning.

Ten of us sat around a table at a cafe in late afternoon sunshine. We'd shed our graduation gowns and caps, and piled into cars to celebrate the official end of high school, forever. Next stop, college. I'd been accepted into the Accounting program at Bentley University in Waltham, Massachusetts, my dad's alma mater.

"Emma." Bridget smacked the plastic tabletop to get my attention. Empty plates rattled against forks and cups. The open umbrella shook, shifting its shadow and making bright sunshine touch her delicate, pale skin. "Are you going to stuff that into your face, or just stare at it?"

"Maybe she thinks it won't hit her thighs if she waits long enough," Tiffany said as she sipped her iced coffee.

I didn't know why I'd come. But I did know I'd paid for the cheesecake in front of me with my own money. Slicing off a bite with my fork, I shrugged. "I'm just not sure I'm hungry." My stomach growled.

Bridget laughed. Her boyfriend joined in. Everyone else followed her lead. My cheeks burned. I stuck the bite into my mouth and tried to savor the delicious, creamy treat. In three months, I'd be on the other side of the country, and I doubted I'd ever see any of these people again. How did I feel about that? I didn't know.

"Who's coming to the beach house tonight?" Bridget's boyfriend asked. Tom leered at me from behind Bridget, like he always did. No one had ever told Bridget how much he hit on the rest of us girls. I couldn't say why, but I didn't want to start now.

"There's going to be a bonfire on the beach," Bridget said, "and Mitch has the key to his dad's liquor cabinet."

"Bikinis required for access to beer," Andy said with a chuckle.

"I guess none of the guys are getting any," Tiffany said. She lifted her nose with a sniff.

"We'll see about that," her boyfriend said. Matt leaned forward to slurp on her ear.

I tuned them out. My bikini fit fine. Probably. Maybe. Sucking in my gut, I held my fork so tight my knuckles turned white. At a public cafe, out in the open, I would not pinch my thighs to check for cellulite. I would not draw attention to my disgusting, fat body.

"Christ," Bridget said as she watched me, "pig at the trough much?"

My cheeks flared again. I swiped the last bite off my fork and set it down, my stomach full of lead and not sure how the cheesecake had disappeared so fast. I'd never fit into my bikini again.

"No wonder you don't have a boyfriend," Tiffany said. She made oinking noises.

Andy waved her off and leered at me. "I'd still hit that."

"You'll hit anything with boobs," Tiffany said.

"Yeah, pretty much." He poked my shoulder, which bothered me, but not enough to do anything more than squirm away. His finger slipped under the slender strap of my lavender minidress to prod the flabby skin between my shoulder bones. "Needs more meat, though. I might break you in half this time."

The guys all leered and grinned like they expected me to strip for them.

Boys didn't know anything. I picked up my plate and stood, though I had no idea what to say. Rather than let loose the wrong thing, I marched myself inside. My belly churned and my neck felt stiff.

"Don't forget to aim," Bridget called after me. She led a new wave of laughter.

My pace quickened with my heart rate, and I hit the bathroom door at a run. Inside, I dashed for the comfort of a stall and knelt before my salvation. The tile cooled my bare knees. I stuck my finger down my throat, like I'd done a thousand times before. I kept my fingernails short and my red hair in a ponytail for this specific reason.

Nothing else gave me the satisfaction or sense of well-being that throwing up did. Though the sensation wracked my body, it purged everything. Worries and fears all went into the magic porcelain bowl. Fat left me. Scorn slid off my shoulders.

I sat up and blew my nose into a wad of toilet paper. After dumping that into the toilet, I stood on wobbly legs and flushed. My vision crowded with static, like it usually did. That and mild dizziness sent me stumbling to the sink, where I splashed water on my face. Twice, I swished water in my mouth and spit it out. The third time, I swallowed a mouthful. Then I toweled my face and dabbed at my makeup.

With that, my ritual ended, and I felt calm. Peaceful. I checked myself in the mirror and nodded with satisfaction. If I never let the food sit in my stomach, it never made me fat. Problem solved. Knowing I'd have to face everyone again, I took a deep breath.

Then again, why did I have to face them? No one could force me to return. I could go home anytime I wanted. They didn't need me to get anywhere. Madison and Andy always rode with me, but they could squeeze into Mark or

Tom's car long enough to get to someone else's place. They could keep their beach beerfest. Beer made guts, and I didn't want one. It caused hangovers, too, and the boys always groped everything in sight.

Holding my head high, I breezed out of the bathroom and through the cafe. As I passed the group, Bridget caught my eye and mimed sticking her finger down her throat. Everyone laughed. I blushed and ran for my car. Last week, they hadn't been so crude. At least, I didn't think so. Maybe I'd gotten fatter somehow.

As I slid behind the wheel of my Beamer, I ran through the list of everything I'd eaten in the past week, discounting what I hadn't digested. One egg for breakfast every day, because I needed protein and didn't like meat. For lunch at school, I had a diet soda, apple, and slice of bread with the rest of the sandwich scraped off. I ate the bottom slice because they always put gross stuff on the top slice, like mayonnaise, mustard, or salad dressing. Sometimes, I had a slice of tomato. Most days, I skipped dinner.

Out of my whole week, I couldn't remember any transgressions I hadn't purged. That wedge of cheese had come back up. So had the ice cream cone with strawberry topping, and the cup of half strawberry sauce, half milk. Oh, God, I hadn't been able to purge the two waffles with strawberry sauce and whipped cream last Sunday with my parents. I rubbed my bloated stomach and started the car. Maybe if I did a hundred sit-ups, I'd be okay.

As I pulled away from the curb, I saw Madison running toward the car. She waved at me. Andy followed on step behind her. I waited. Madison opened the door.

"Hey, are you okay?" She bent to see me. Her blonde ringlets framed her perfect face. She looked so good in her watermelon skater dress and white sandals that I wanted to hate her. I liked her anyway.

Andy pushed the passenger seat forward and slid into the back. He fit by sitting sideways with his feet on the seat.

"What're you ditching us for?"

"I just want to go home," I said. As soon as Madison climbed in and shut the door, I pulled into traffic. Boutiques and cafes lined the road, with a layer of on-street parking on both sides. Flower pots hung from the lampposts and a banner had been strung across the road to congratulate us all for completing our term of suffering in high school.

"Can I come over?" Andy asked.

"Of course you can," Madison said. "Right? Your parents aren't there."

If I took them home, Andy would try to get one or both of us in bed with him, and I wasn't in the mood. "I'm pretty tired," I said.

"Aw, c'mon, Emma." Andy slipped his hand around the seat to my shoulder. His fingers rubbed my arm and neck at the same time. "You say that and it sounds like you don't like us anymore."

I squirmed. Swirling static crept into my vision. I hated when that happened outside of the bathroom. The car swerved. Madison screamed. Andy snatched back his hand. I slammed on the brakes and cranked the wheel. My heart pounded and my vision cleared. We missed hitting an oncoming car by inches.

"Jesus," Andy said. "Keep your eyes on the road! You'll get us all killed."

Panting, I kept my hands on the wheel and thanked God nothing had happened. The other driver flipped me off as he passed, which I deserved. I stared at the road, determined to get home without crashing.

CHAPTER 2

"Maybe we should go to my place," Madison said. Out of the corner of my eye, I could tell she watched me.

After that screw-up, I'd watch me too. "Yeah," I said. My left leg wouldn't stop bouncing. I thought my hands might shake if I let go of the wheel.

"Whatever," Andy said.

We left the downtown core in favor of the suburbs. Trees lined the roads and carved signs marked the entrances to named neighborhoods. Madison and I lived in the same one, with a large, blinding white sign painted with sparkling gold letters—Blithewood. Every spring, the HOA had the stupid sign redone.

Madison lived near the entrance. I pulled into the driveway of her parents' two-story house with sculpted shrubs and manicured grass. Madison hopped out, showing her dimples. Andy climbed out. I sat in the car.

"Aren't you coming in?" Madison asked, her smile fading around the edges. Her gaze flicked toward Andy as if to beg me not to leave her alone with him.

I hated myself for abandoning her. But I did it anyway. "I'm pretty tired. I think I should just go home and take a nap. Don't want to conk out at the beach party, right?"

"Aw, c'mon, Emma," Andy whined. "Come inside. Lie down here."

"No, thanks." I put the car in reverse.

Madison sighed and shut the door. I backed into the street and tried to ignore the way her shoulders slumped as she turned to face Andy. He shrugged and draped an arm around her. And then I plunged deeper into the neighborhood, leaving them behind.

My house had three stories and a four-car garage. A small army of gardeners took care of our expansive yard, keeping it tidy, weed-free, and bursting with flowers as often as possible. I parked on my side of the garage, next to the spot that should have been Ethan's. Instead, Dad had filled it with boxes of holiday decoration stuff that otherwise would've gone into the attic every year. Why bother hauling it up and down the ladder when he didn't have to?

Inside, the house was silent. My shoes clunked on the hardwood floor, which echoed off the walls and the cathedral ceiling in the living room. Never-opened books lay on the coffee table, in front of a couch only company got to use. Art I didn't like hung on all the walls, except for one framed photograph.

As I often did, I stopped in front of Ethan's smiling picture and tapped the glass with my pink fingernails. In the picture, he was seventeen, fresh out of high school. He wore his dress uniform and stood in front of an American flag. By now, he would've been twenty-three. My sigh seemed to fill the huge room and bounce back to press on my shoulders.

I padded into the kitchen and fetched myself a glass of ice water, which helped curb my hunger pangs. The day was warm or I would've heated it for even better suppression. The water came with me to the third floor. Two bedrooms, a large shared space, and a giant bathroom took up the floor. Ethan had shared it with me. His taste still dominated the shared area.

Posters of starscapes, the space shuttle, and the moon covered the walls. Early space program craft hung from wires —Vostok 1, Freedom 7, Mercury with an attached Atlas rocket, Gemini, and Apollo. Mom and Dad had never approved of his yearning for space, so we'd built the models together using printouts he found online. I'd cut out the paper pieces and he'd glue them to cardboard to make the shapes. His last birthday before he left, I'd saved enough allowance to get a genuine plastic and metal model kit of a Soyuz capsule. The finished product sat alone on a shelf beside the TV.

We'd both agreed on the posters of Hedy Lamarr and Diana Rigg as Emma Peel in The Avengers. Lamarr had brains and Rigg had brawn. Both had beauty. Modern actresses had nothing on either of those fine ladies. Ethan had agreed.

I needed something distracting to do, so I fetched my small toolbox from its shelf in my closet and sat at my desk. Pieces of gray plastic covered a mat over the wood surface. For a challenge, I'd bought five different space and air models, then catalogued the parts and designed my own custom starship with them.

Because that was my dream. Ethan wanted to go to Mars, and I wanted to build the things to get him there. Mom and Dad might've been more excited about my graduation today if my grades had been worth crowing about. Two point five three had been all I could scrape. Instead of doing my homework, I'd spent hours poring over calculus, physics, and engineering, figuring it out with help from videos by obscure scientists. While all my friends had played games and climbed into each other's pants, I'd learned to use CAD and wind-modeling software.

Math should have been my strength, but Algebra had bored me to tears when I'd already spent hours and hours coming to understand differentials and circuit diagrams on my own terms. Someday, when I wasn't fat and disgusting anymore, I'd find a way to get an interview at the Jet Propulsion Laboratories. They'd see my smarts and initiative, and my designs would impress them. The fantasy ended with me presenting my finished custom model with a bright smile.

With needlenose pliers, glue, an anchored clamp arm,

and a tiny screwdriver, I added another few parts to my masterpiece. Nothing else mattered. Details slid into place and my design came together, bit by bit. Each tiny panel or widget had a place. I measured twice and glued once.

When I had to pause to use the bathroom, I checked the clock. The beach party started in two hours.

I whirred into panic mode. Had I done any sit-ups when I got home? No. How did I expect to fit into my bikini?

Leaving my tools sitting out like a slob, I dropped to the floor and cranked through crunches as fast as I could. Somewhere in the middle, I lost count. I must've done fifty or sixty before I had to stop to catch my breath and wait for the static to recede. After that, I did a thousand jumping jacks. By the time I stopped, buckets of sweat oozed from my pores. Gross.

Showering made me feel better. It always did. Water sluiced away grime and erased evidence of anything. I could cry in the shower and no one ever knew.

Giant, frosted globe lights cast soft, yellow-white light across the tiled expanse of my bathroom. I stared at my damp self in the mirror with a grimace of disgust. Bulges and flab hung everywhere. Shadows under my eyes made me look like a freak. My nose had broken out in blackheads again, probably because of the cheesecake. I hadn't purged it fast enough.

Wrapping my pink, fluffy robe around my body let me not look at it anymore. I didn't need to see my gut bulges. No one wanted to see that. When I wore my bikini, everyone would. The one-piece swimsuit in the drawer with my bikini sounded like a good idea. Facing the choice of being laughed at for my gut and being laughed at for the extra fabric, I liked the option that took more effort to remove.

I sighed and attacked my hair, resigned to the judgment of my friends. Unlike Madison's tight, elegant curls, my mop frizzed into a puff when I did nothing to it. Step one had me dragging a comb through it, teasing out the snarls.

That fact kept me out of the water at the beach.

As I watched my gross, knobby hands work with my tangles, my vision clouded with swirling motes of static. This time, though, instead of filling my sight, it only covered the mirror. When I turned my head, everything else seemed fine. The surface of the mirror writhed with dancing black and white dots.

Maybe I'd passed out in the shower? The dots jerked sideways in a flicker, forming a fleeting picture of Ethan with his mouth moving. Except he looked older, with more muscle and his face and shoulders filled out. He looked like an adult, like a soldier from a movie. I reached a hand for him. The static returned.

"No! Come back! Don't leave me again!" I lurched forward and pounded on the mirror, my eyes burning with tears.

I couldn't go through that again. The knock on the door, the colonel sitting in our living room. Papers. The word "classified," over and over. Mom falling apart. Dad telling me to go to my room. When I don't go, Mom screams at me.

They couldn't give us a flag because they never found his body.

"Please," I begged the mirror.

The static flickered. I fell forward.

CHAPTER 3

I flew through something cold and wet to land in a heap on an industrial tile floor. The impact stunned me.

"Miss Harper," a man said. I recognized Mr. Mackie's disappointed sigh.

My cheeks flared with a red-hot blush as I realized my robe didn't cover me. I tugged it over my butt and squirmed to sit up without flashing the school principal more than I already had.

Dark blue lockers lined a side hallway of my high school. Fluorescent lights buzzed overhead. Nearby, other students passed in the main hallway. Every boy I saw grinned at me like he'd seen everything before I shut my robe. All the girls hid laughter behind their hands.

"You're not dressed appropriately for school, Miss Harper." Mr. Mackie's thick eyebrows flared across his forehead.

Holding my robe shut with sausage-fat fingers, I stood and raised my chin as high as I could manage. The flesh under my jaw jiggled. "I don't care. I graduated already."

Mr. Mackie sighed again. "It's lunch time, Miss Harper. You should run along to the cafeteria."

I turned my back on him and hurried to the front doors. He had no authority over me anymore. This place had no authority over me anymore. Bright sunshine glowed through the glass and glinted off the floor. When I tossed the left door open, I stepped over the threshold and into the one place I never wanted to go—the cafeteria.

Everyone watched me. Heat flared across my face and down my neck.

My favorite part of school lunch, the salad bar, beckoned. Vegetables didn't make anyone fat. I shuffled to it and piled my plate high with lettuce, tomatoes, olives, mushrooms, cucumbers, and carrots. Four vats of thick, creamy salad dressing waited at the end like trolls lurking under a bridge.

Bridget leaned past me to ladle salad dressing onto my plate. I hadn't seen her coming. She made oinking noises as she drenched my vegetables. I moved my plate. The dressing splashed onto my robe.

She laughed. "Aw, look at that. Such a waste. I guess you'll have to lick it up, princess."

I salivated at the idea. Then I recoiled in disgust at myself. "Gross."

Behind me, Andy chuckled, low and throaty. "I'll do it."

I spun, flinging vegetables and dressing everywhere. Instead of Andy, I found a wolf-person. He stood on his hind legs, both bent the wrong way. Gray and white fur covered every inch of him, though he wore black pants, boots, and a vest. He had a wolf-like snout and icy blue eyes. Instead of two thick, muscular arms ending with claw-tipped fingers, he had one metal arm. The obvious prosthetic mirrored the shape of his real arm aside from the fur, and had more complex articulation than anything I'd ever seen.

He reminded me of furry anime.

His fake hand raised a thick, boxy gun to point at me. I threw the empty plate at him. He flinched. I ran.

My robe flapped open as I dashed through the doors. Holding it shut, I kept running up the hallway to my locker. Why was I even at school? I graduated. We had the ceremony.

Mr. Mackie shook my hand and congratulated me. My parents took pictures, then they left so I could hang out with my friends.

I turned a corner. Another wolfman stood in front of my locker. This one had cybernetics replacing part of his face and one eye. The eye glowed red and I could see the iris shrink as he focused on me. This wolf held a rifle with a strip of glowing green down the barrel. He sniffed the air and swiped his tongue across his muzzle.

The salad dressing gave me away as his target.

He took a step toward me and raised his rifle. "Come here, little girl," he said with Tom's voice.

Darting across the intersection, I caught a bright glow of green from the rifle, then felt blinding heat sear across my back. Without checking over my shoulder, I ran as fast as I could.

Green bolts vaporized spots on the floor, creating potholes in a line beside me. I dove into the open door of the art studio. My feet tangled in a sea of paintbrushes, charcoal, and loose canvas. I fell to the floor and scrambled to reach the back of the room. The art studio had an emergency exit to the outside.

But I couldn't leave. I had to get to my locker. Something inside my locker would save me. It would save everyone. If I could just reach my locker, everything would be fine. Forever.

Save me from what? The wolfpeople, I guessed. Why did school have wolfpeople? Had aliens invaded while I took my shower? Why invade my school?

Wait. Because it had the thing inside my locker. They wanted it. I had to protect it. If I protected it, that thing I couldn't picture or name would save us all. Somehow.

None of this made sense. The bathroom mirror had drawn me into something not physically possible.

Unless I died and this was Hell. I might've slipped in the shower and cracked my head open. My parents had said they planned to go out for the evening, so they wouldn't find me until much too late. No one else would find me either.

Or I could've fallen into some kind of in-between, and what I did decided how I spent eternity. Why else would I have an obsession with my locker? The pre-packaged bran muffins in there wouldn't save anything. They couldn't even save me from thunder thighs, let alone some unknown doom.

I reached the outside door, intending to circle around and use the front entrance. Throwing it open, I braced to run barefoot across pavement. Instead, it shifted me to the front lobby. This somehow made sense, even though it didn't. Whatever I'd fallen into, I wanted it to stop. How did I make it stop? By reaching my locker.

Bright sunshine streamed over my bloated, gross shoulders, gleaming off the tile as I faced the hallway between the main office and Student Support.

My shadow reminded me of a wad of marshmallows stuck together.

Two new wolfmen stood at the next hall intersection. One had a cybernetic leg, the other had all his original parts and wore dark goggles. They held rifles and watched me, blocking the easiest path to my locker. I ducked inside the office. They wouldn't know where all the doors led. None of them had spent four years disappointing every teacher and Mr. Mackie, then slipping out to hide in a dark corner.

I reached a door and stopped with my hand on the knob. Anyone could see a door. Even if they didn't know which door I used, it would still open and shut, and the wolfpeople only had to stand where they could see it. With their laser rifles, they could shoot me from a distance.

Backing away from the door, I scanned the office. It had desks, chairs, computers, doors, potted plants, and…air ducts. As I turned toward the nearest vent, the door I'd almost used exploded in a haze of green.

Panic surging through me, I darted into Mr. Mackie's office. He sat in his chair and looked up from a folder. His

16

eyebrows swished, the thick, long hairs dancing in a breeze I couldn't feel.

"Miss Harper, we should discuss your GPA and what it means for college admissions."

My robe swirled around me as I stopped. The ranch dressing hit me in the face and made me nauseous. I swiped a hand across my face and shook my hand to fling white stuff against the walls and floor. "How can you not hear the explosions?"

"Explosions? Don't change the subject, Miss Harper. You got a D in Chemistry."

I wanted to cry. The day before midterms, I'd passed out in gym class and Mom made me stay home for three days. Our school's anti-cheating policy meant I had to take special tests, nothing like the ones everybody else. All the teachers decided I must've faked it and gave me crazy questions. The only subject I'd passed had been math, and only because the math teacher had given me questions two years above my grade level.

"I know the periodic table. That test wasn't fair!"

"It's a hard lesson to learn, Miss Harper, that life is not fair."

A green bolt flew into the room. It missed me and hit Mr. Mackie's head. Blood and gore spattered my face. Except it didn't smell right. The gore smelled sweet and creamy. He'd exploded into…cheesecake covered with strawberry sauce?

I swiped a finger across my cheek and licked it. Mr. Mackie was made of strawberry cheesecake. Despite knowing a wolfperson must have found me, I crossed the room and touched Mr. Mackie's neck. Strawberry sauce dribbled out the center of his neck and down the front of his suit.

Before I knew what to think, I'd grabbed a huge gob of cheesecake and stuffed it into my mouth like a greedy pig. I heard Bridget's oinking noises.

"Don't forget to aim," she called.

Tiffany echoed the oinks.

I had to get away from the cheesecake principal.

My hands, face, and robe smeared with strawberry sauce, I threw myself at the air vent in Mr. Mackie's office. The flimsy metal bent inward. I stuck my fingers through the distorted holes and tugged. Nothing happened. Me and my pathetic muscles couldn't do anything worthwhile. Ever.

The Andy wolfman stepped into the doorway. He didn't have a gun anymore. Instead, he had a dark, malicious grin. He pointed his gun at me. "Yeah, I'd totally hit that again."

Nothing worked against Andy except passing him off on someone else.

I had no one else.

CHAPTER 4

Screwing my eyes shut, I huddled against the wall and waited. My shoulders shook, jiggling the fat all over my body.

Instead of Andy the wolfman grabbing or hitting me, I heard laughter. Bridget, Tiffany, Tom, Andy, and all the rest of the guys laughed at me. I lowered my hands.

Fire flickered in the darkness of a starry night. Waves crashed nearby. Everyone writhed in a crowd of bodies around the bonfire. On the fringes of the light, beer bottles, beach chairs, and coolers sat in the sand.

Somehow, I'd missed driving myself to the beach party. I couldn't remember losing that much time before. Usually, the static took a few seconds at most. Usually, I remembered the static coming and watched it recede. Usually didn't seem to matter in this time and place.

I wore my bikini. No wonder everyone laughed. Fat rippled everywhere, unconstrained by the lavender strings and fabric. In my usual clothes, no one cared. Like this, everyone saw it. I wondered if my head would explode from blushing.

Crossing my arms helped. A little.

Wolfman arms—one cybered and one furry—wrapped around me from behind. "Nice of you to join us," Andy murmured into my ear. His fur brushed my cheek, my neck my back, my legs.

Panic made me freeze. I couldn't move. I couldn't speak. I couldn't breathe.

Bridget and Tiffany stepped in front of the crowd, radiant and perfect in their red and orange bikinis, respectively. Madison sat in a beach chair, huddled under a huge towel. I shouldn't have abandoned her. We could've worked together to keep Andy busy with other things for hours.

"Did you remember to aim?" Bridget asked.

Everyone laughed. Andy licked my neck.

At a time like this, I expected the static to come. It didn't. Why not? The static never came in dreams, I knew that much. This felt too real for a dream. In dreams, I never felt like I had any control over what happened. The vision played itself and I danced like a marionette. This thing, whatever I'd gotten lost inside, let me do what I wanted.

If this wasn't real and also wasn't a dream, what was it?

The wolfman version of Tom stepped in front of Bridget and Tiffany, holding a laser gun. "Stop playing with your food."

Andy growled in the back of his throat. He pressed his claws against my flesh hard enough to scratch through a layer of skin. Drops of blood welled in the tiny, stinging wounds. "She's so…delicious."

The wolfmen wanted to eat me if I didn't get the thing in my locker. Except the beach house was nowhere near school. Why had I left school without getting to my locker? Didn't something in there matter?

Why had we all abandoned the thing I needed to protect? Why couldn't I name that thing?

Out of the corner of my eye, I noticed a thin glow peeking from the largest cooler on the sand. The thing in my locker had moved to the cooler. Somehow.

"God, Emma." Bridget sneered at me. "It takes a real pig for them to want to eat you."

Andy licked the blood on my chest. I squirmed. He clamped his paw against me harder.

"Wiggle more. Like prey." His voice slithered across my skin, quiet and dark. His other paws lifted a handful of something white with red goo to my face.

The heady scent of strawberry drenched cheesecake hit me like a brick. Andy shoved the pawful of delight into my mouth. But I didn't want it. He never gave me anything I wanted. Andy only cared about what Andy wanted.

Closing my eyes again, I crumpled. Fighting Andy never worked. Fighting wolfmen stronger than the guys in my life wouldn't work.

Andy let me fall. Everyone laughed. Strawberry cheesecake hit my back. I huddled on myself and spat out what I could.

As I stuck my finger into my mouth, Andy's hot breath pressed against my neck. "Fight, Emma," he whispered. "Get up and fight."

Like a pathetic coward, I sputtered and cried. "I can't."

"Get up."

I flinched at his harsh command and curled into a ball. My body shuddered as I wept.

"Get up, Emma! Get up now or I'll kill you!"

Some kind of fire exploded in my belly. I looked up and screamed at him. "Then kill me! I can't stand this anymore! Just do it already! I'm never going to do anything I want, so it doesn't matter and nobody cares anyway!"

Andy, Tom, and other wolfpeople crowded around me. One wore Bridget's bikini, her fur precise and smooth around it.

"That's right, princess. Nobody cares." Bridget leaned down. I wanted to punch her in the snout, but I didn't know how to punch anyone. If I tried, she'd probably bite my hand off. "No one is coming to save you."

Tiffany the wolf dragged Madison into view by the arm. Madison wore a one-piece swimsuit in a blue that matched her eyes. Her hair hung in perfect curls. I'd seen her crying enough times to recognize the red and puffiness.

I met her gaze and didn't know what to say. Abandoning her gnawed at me. We should've shoved Andy aside and hung out together. Why didn't I do that? I didn't know. "I'm sorry."

Tiffany kicked me in the side. "Nobody cares! Get up and fight or we kill her."

Tom pressed the barrel of his gun against Madison's head. Madison's eyes widened. I stared with no idea what to do. They wanted me to fight, but I didn't know how, and I didn't want to fight.

The gun fired. Bright green light flared against Madison's head. Her body spasmed. I opened my mouth and made no sound. She closed her eyes and fell to the sand. I reached for her.

Andy grabbed me and lifted me into the air. I didn't resist. How could I? Why would I? Nothing mattered anymore. I wanted to die.

"This is your fault." Bridget nudged Madison's limp body with her furry foot. "You could've saved her. But you didn't. Because you're a worthless, fatass brat. Maybe if you got up and did something, you wouldn't be so pathetic."

I had nothing to say for myself. They were right. Letting myself go limp, I waited for whatever they decided to do.

"Waste of space," Tom said.

The arms holding me let go. I hit the sand. Tom grabbed a hunk of my hair and pulled my head up. He pressed the barrel of his gun to my forehead.

Green light filled my vision.

I opened my eyes and gasped for breath. Someone with thick muscles ran with me slung over a shoulder. My arms dangled toward an unfamiliar, metal grate floor, and I wore my robe again. Harsh red light flashed off walls of bare sheet metal. The person carrying me wore dark clothes and boots, and didn't seem furry.

We turned a corner, and I caught glimpses of two human men following me. Both also wore dark clothing and boots. They carried sleek rifles and had short hair. One had tanned skin, the other dusky. Neither paid attention to me.

Not sure if I hallucinated or what, I waited for the wolfpeople to show up and torment me again. Because they would. I knew they would.

"Baldwin, where's my hole?" the man carrying me shouted.

All three men stumbled as something rocked the ground. The one carrying me bounced into a wall and seemed intent on protecting me from harm.

"Left!" another man shouted from ahead. I figured this for Baldwin.

"She's awake," one of the men behind us said, his deep, Southern drawl coming through despite my confusion.

"Hang on, Cog," the man carrying me said. His baritone voice sounded like Ethan, which made no sense. My heart fluttered anyway, because no one else used that nickname.

Whether Ethan carried me or I only dreamed it, I had no reason to resist. I did everything I could to make myself easy to carry. Holding onto his pants kept me steady, and I didn't wiggle to get a better look at anything.

We rounded a corner and Probably-Ethan leaped over a ridge. We passed through a chill and I saw an impossible number of stars for a moment, then we landed on a hard, brown floor surrounded by red-brown walls. Veins of blue-white light spidered across the walls, offering enough illumination to see the tunnel we rushed through.

"Akata!" probably-Ethan shouted. "Get us out of here!"

My vision fuzzed with static, and I groaned as nausea rolled over me. I felt like my whole being shifted a step to the left without me moving. We rolled sideways. I blacked out.

23

CHAPTER 5

I awoke in a small, cozy space. Soft white light showed me red-brown walls the color of dried blood, close enough to call a cocoon. Tiny, irregular lines on the surface provided the light. Despite having no blanket, I felt warm, and the surface beneath me felt like memory foam. Not sure if I needed to panic or not, I lifted my hands.

The walls parted at my touch. More red-brown walls with more white tendrils formed a larger room with a narrow doorway. I sat up, still wearing my robe. The pod-like thing holding me had four identical copies in a line, each attached to the wall and floor. If I wanted to climb out, my feet would reach the floor without me having to straighten my legs.

"Cog, don't panic," probably-Ethan said. His voice sounded distant, like he shouted from another room. "I'll be there in a minute."

Panic swelled in my chest. I jumped out of the pod and scrambled to get away from it. When I reached the doorway, my shoulders hit the walls and the opening widened. I fell to the floor. The solid surface shared the same dead blood color as the walls, but had no veins.

I couldn't breathe. Nothing made sense. I'd passed out in the shower, hit my head, and died. And I'd gone to Hell.

"Whoa, whoa." Ethan crouched beside me and flipped my robe shut. "Calm down." He wrapped his arms around me and held me close. "I know you're confused. I'm sorry about that. It was an accident."

I burst into tears. Wracking sobs exploded from me, and I didn't know how to stop them. Ethan made soothing noises and rubbed my back. I didn't want to die. I'd never wanted to die. And I'd always believed Ethan survived somehow. Both of us in Hell together made everything so much worse.

"Hey, Cog. It's okay. You're gonna be okay." He brushed my hair like he used to do.

"I don't want to be dead," I sobbed. Sitting on his lap, in the circle of his thick, muscular arms reminded me of times before he left.

A nightmare had sent me running to him, not Mom and Dad. We sat on his bed, him holding eight-year-old me and promising the demon adding machine couldn't hurt me.

"You're not," he murmured. "You didn't die. We're in a different part of the universe, but we're not dead."

"What?" I pulled away and wiped my face on my sleeve. I thought I smelled ranch dressing. Ugh.

Ethan huffed. "It's a long story. The most important thing is I didn't mean to drag you here. We thought we'd be able to send a message through with that gizmo. The rest can wait. You need clothes, and maybe some water to splash on your face?"

My stomach growled, a boomerang and a traitor rolled into one. "Yeah. Okay."

"And food. I can feed you." He pointed at the open gap leading to the five pods. "That's the sleep chamber. Akata can make you a separate one if you want, but it really doesn't matter much when you're in a pod."

I took his help to stand on wobbly legs. "I don't need food."

"Don't be ridiculous. Your stomach growled." He squeezed my hand. It hurt. "Akata, Emma needs markers."

The wall beside me made a squidgy, slimy noise. At my

eye level, white veins wriggled to the surface like sticky worms and formed a shape like a sideways lightning bolt. Not sure I believed Ethan about our life status, I kept watching as the glow shifted until it formed three Zs.

Words failed me. I blinked at it, then at Ethan.

He grinned with his clean-shaven, square jaw. "For sleep."

I couldn't decide which was more surreal—this or the cyborg wolfmen at school and the beach.

Ethan tugged me down the hall, his stride strong and full of purpose. I shambled in his wake, bent over and doing my best not to fall on my face. We didn't go far before he stopped in front of another symbol made of veins, this one in the shape of pants. He touched the wall beside the shape, and a gap opened on a small, empty room. It had enough space for a single person to stand.

He urged me inside. "This will be weird, but don't be scared."

"Weird? What'll be weird?" I balked at the threshold.

Smiling with more confidence than I'd ever felt in my whole life, he shooed me through the gap. "Akata, Emma needs a uniform."

"What?" I had no good reason to resist him, just confusion. As soon as I passed through the gap, the two halves sealed me inside. I froze.

The walls squished around me. I tried to scream and had no idea why no sound came out of my mouth. Though the surface seemed bumpy and rough, when it touched my skin, it reminded me of memory foam again. Warm and soft, it enveloped my body from my neck down. The sensation reminded me of…nothing. I had no frame of reference for being wrapped in something this encompassing and comforting.

For at least fifty beats of my thumping heart, the walls kept me in their grasp. Light, gentle massage touched every square inch of me. Then it withdrew. Soft, smooth black fabric covered my body, and I wore black boots, just like Ethan's. Wiggling my toes, I could tell I wore socks. How had it done that? I patted my butt and found the edges of a pair of underwear. The shirt included support for my small bust. The whole goth emo outfit clung to my grotesque shape, from the closed collar at the base of my neck to the narrow holes for my wrists and ankles.

"I don't suppose this can be white? Or pink? Maybe lavender?"

"Jesus," Ethan muttered, "have Mom and Dad been starving you?"

I turned to see him frowning at me through the open gap. "What?"

He reached in and took my hand to pull me out. "I can see your ribs. That's not normal."

My cheeks burned and I couldn't look at him. "I know I'm a fat pig."

"Who the hell told you that? You're not a fat pig, you're way too skinny."

Once again, my stomach rumbled. "I'm not skinny at all."

"You're *gaunt*." Shaking his head, he tugged me along the hallway again. "Never mind. This is the Mess."

We stopped at an already-open gap with a vein shape of a fork. Inside, the wall-stuff formed a table with five stool-like chairs. The other men occupied three of them, eating what looked like vegetable lo mein out of white bowls with metal forks. They chewed with slurping and crunching noises.

"Guys, this is Emma. Emma, this is Baldwin, Nash, and Mendez."

All four men had the same build—broad shoulders, square jaws, and thick muscles. Baldwin was white, Nash was black, and Mendez fell in between. From his name, I guessed Hispanic. The three of them nodded to me. I couldn't decide which one was the most handsome. They all seemed so confident and competent, even doing something as mundane as eating.

"Marines don't talk with their mouths full," Ethan said. He pushed me at a chair.

I sat next to Mendez and tried not to stare at them, or at anything else. "Hi." How did I even start any kind of conversation? We sat in cushy chairs made from animate goo the color of dried blood, apparently in some foreign part of the universe, the four of them missing and presumed dead for two years. Had Mom and Dad come home and noticed me missing yet? Would they ever notice?

Ethan set a bowl and fork in front of me, then sat beside me with one of his own. "Eat."

The food smelled a lot like chicken soup. "I'm not hungry." My stomach growled yet again. I hated it.

All four men paused in the act of scooping food into their mouths to stare at me.

"Eat," Ethan repeated.

Mendez picked up my fork and stuck it in my hand. "Chica, you don't pass up a chance to eat when you got it." Though he used a Spanish word, he had a Midwestern non-accent with his tenor voice.

Ethan shoved a wad of noodle and colored bits into his mouth and raised an eyebrow at me as if to ask why I didn't follow suit.

I poked the food with the fork. The short, yellowish, noodle-like things moved like noodles. Among them, colored bits reminded me of chopped vegetables, but I couldn't identify anything. "What is it?"

"Food," Baldwin said.

"But what kind?" Noodles had no nutritional value for me. I ate protein as my number one priority, and avoided carbs at all costs. Protein fueled muscles. Carbs made fat.

Nash shrugged. "Noodle bowl." He had a light Southern accent and a deep, rich voice. For some reason, that made everything seem more real.

Mendez took my hand and stabbed some of my food

with the fork I held. His touch startled me enough to jerk my shoulders. No one seemed to notice my reaction. "Protein, fiber, carbs, fat, and other stuff you need to survive. Tastes about like it smells."

I shrank away from something with fat in it. "I don't want it."

"This is what we've got," Ethan said. I could tell his patience waned. "No one dies of starvation on my watch while we have food."

Not wanting to aggravate him so soon after getting him back, I stared at the noodle bowl and swished my fork through it. The food smelled good, and I didn't have any other options. I stuck the fork into my mouth. Like Mendez said, it tasted like it smelled. One bite full of mushy and crunchy made me whimper with how much I liked it. To avoid watching the men watch me, I gave the bowl my attention and shoveled food into my face.

"See?" Mendez said. "It's fine. Nothing to shout about, but fine."

"Get used to noodle bowl, Cog, because we eat it a lot." Great.

CHAPTER 6

We took the empty bowls and used spoons to a hole in the red-brown stuff and dropped them in. Ethan patted the side of the hole after I dropped mine in, and the hole sealed itself shut. It sealed so well, I couldn't tell it had ever been a hole.

"What is this place?"

Ethan put an arm around my shoulders and led me out of the room with the other men. "Akata."

I waited for more words. None came. "Oh, well, that explains everything. Now I understand. It's so obvious. How could I have been confused at all?"

Mendez laughed. Nash and Baldwin chuckled. Ethan squeezed my shoulder. It hurt.

"Akata is sort of a brain overseeing a colony of blood coral," Ethan said. "So, basically, we're inside a coral reef in space."

"A coral reef. In space." I wanted to hit him. "So I'm dead, and Hell is you explaining things without explaining them."

We entered a large room with five chairs in a line, all facing a dark, smooth wall. This wall was made of something different than the rest of the ship. It reminded me of a giant, flatscreen TV. Ethan pushed me into a chair on the end. Mendez sat beside me, and Ethan took the center chair.

"Akata, show us what's outside," Ethan said.

The dark wall flashed into a picture with amazing clarity. Bright spots of color dotted the velvety black expanse. We moved toward a yellow dot about the size of my fist, and passed something big and blue to the left.

"Man, I love this view," Mendez murmured.

I agreed. Though I didn't recognize any constellations, seeing the stars without light pollution to conceal them never failed to soothe me. Rarely did have the chance to lie someplace and stare at the night sky uninterrupted.

Ethan gestured to the screen. "We have no idea where we are. None of us studied enough astronomy to have a guess. That means we have no idea how to get home. Even if we did know which direction to go, Akata only goes so fast. We'll probably die of old age before we reach Earth."

"We're stuck out here? Forever?" I blinked. The mirror had taken me away from home forever? Instead of my parents who didn't care, my friends who called me names and seemed to hate me, and a college degree I didn't want, I got my brother and his friends in space coral.

"And that makes you happy," Ethan said with a frown.

I hadn't realized how broadly I smiled until he said that. "There's nothing to go to home to."

"Maybe not for you," Nash said. "The rest of us got families. People we care about."

"I'm sorry," I said. My cheeks burned and I hung my head. "I didn't mean— Sorry."

"Guys," Ethan said, "go do something. I'll explain things to my sister."

"Yes, Sergeant," Nash, Mendez, and Baldwin intoned together. They left us alone. Mendez patted my shoulder on his way out.

Ethan turned in his chair, and it swiveled to accommodate him. He leaned forward and clasped his hands, resting his arms on his knees. His stare fell halfway between exasperation and annoyance. "We decided a while ago that our mission is to return to Earth by whatever means we can manage. There's one option we're pretty sure of, which is what we were trying to do when you fell through to here."

"I didn't mean that I wouldn't help us all get home," I murmured. Part of me had a hard time accepting the reality of this situation. The rest of me wanted to dance and sing about my new freedom.

"I know." Ethan sighed and rubbed his face. He sat back and stopped looking at me. "We've been out here for a long time, Cog. We've met some other species, but none of them are friendly. There were twelve of us when we started—a full squad. Eight men have died out here. This is a harsh part of the universe for humans. You can't mess around if you want to survive."

"It doesn't seem dangerous."

"No, not right now. Akata is taking us out of range of the transmission station sentinels."

Like the time at school and on the beach with the wolfpeople, this felt so real and so fake at the same time. "This seems too much like a dream. You went missing. They came to the house and told us there was no hope." I flashed on Mom wailing. She missed Ethan. Maybe Dad did too, but he never showed it. "Then I never got another letter."

"I'm sorry for that. We didn't come here by choice. You saw some people you know in a place you've been, then some cyborg wolfmen when you came across, right? And the wolfmen attacked or goaded you?"

Stunned by his knowledge, I nodded and had no idea what to say.

"It happened to all of us too. We landed in that facility and robots herded us." He stared at the floor and recited in a monotone. "The robots stuffed guns in our hands and shoved us into a box. The box shifted. Kidd threw up and we couldn't do anything about it." He rubbed his eyes with a finger and thumb. "We've fought the wolfmen and half a dozen other types of aliens a hundred times at this point. They want us dead, and I have no idea why. We can't communicate with them. Whoever brought us here hasn't given us any idea what we're supposed to do except fight those wolfmen."

"That's awful." I touched his knee because I couldn't imagine the situation he'd described.

He nodded and sighed. "Yes. The important part, though, is we're sure we can use that transmission station to get home. It brought us here, so there's got to be a way for it to get us back. There are two main problems. One, the sentinels. We're not sure exactly what they detect, but when they come online, they attack the station to get us. So far as we can tell, they can't detect Akata.

"The second problem is the one that just caught you. It seems to be programmed to bring things from Earth to here, and not the other way around. Even if we knew how to change that, the station robots spend all their time trying to stuff us into a box, so we have to defend against that. Today was the first time we reached the mission room, so maybe it's easy, but we need more time to figure it out."

On the off chance this was real and not Hell, I nodded and thought about the problem. "Is the transmission station like Akata?"

"No, it's all metal and electronics. We don't know who built it, but it'd fit into any space movie I ever saw." He turned to the screen. "Akata, show us a picture of the transmission station."

The screen showed an image of a long, tubular hunk of metal centered in a star field. Sections protruded as if it had some part too large for the main tube to hold. Circles with thin, blue lights streaked across the entire length surrounding the whole tube like rings, anchored to the central tube by a strange flickering phenomenon. I stood and approached the screen, trying to understand what I saw. The space between the central tube and the rings reminded me of airplane propellers at night.

"Are those rings spinning?"

"Yes." Ethan stood beside me. "It uses them to generate gravity, though I have no idea why. The robots don't need gravity, and humans would be easier to herd without it."

I shrugged because I had no answer for something like that. For all I knew, humans had built the station. Somehow. "It might be a simple matter of reversing something. I mean, I have no idea how you create a wormhole, but maybe if I saw the plans or something, I could figure out what to switch to send us back."

"You?"

I nudged him with an elbow. "Yeah, me. I didn't stop wanting to build spaceships just because you gave up on becoming an astronaut."

"I didn't give up," he muttered.

"You had a funny way of showing it. Since you decided not to learn how to fly planes. Joining the Marines instead of the Air Force didn't exactly seem like the logical choice either."

Ethan crossed his arms. "I was hoping to get in through one of the expertise paths."

"Getting shot at in a barren wasteland on the other side of the planet helped a ton with that, I'm sure." The barb seemed too strong, like I thought he'd enlisted to spite me. Did I? Maybe?

"Settle down." He draped an arm around my shoulders and tugged me into a hug. "I missed you, Cog."

Like he'd flipped a switch, tears flooded my eyes. "I missed you too."

CHAPTER 7

"This is it," Ethan said as he stopped in front of a vein symbol of several dots. "There's not much more to the ship. It's not very big, which is probably why the sentinels ignore her. Akata brings our supplies out when we need them, so there's no human access to the cargo hold. Otherwise, there's Akata herself, and she's delicate. Porter sneezed at her once and she couldn't fly for a week. So we don't go down there. She interfaces with us through the sleep pods."

"Wait. What? She interfaces? Like…" The first time I'd made out with Andy, he'd been all about interfacing.

Ethan rolled his eyes. "*Brain* interface. It's why she understands us and we know the ship is made of blood coral. She'll try to help you in whatever way she can. We don't have nightmares. Not terrible ones, anyway."

I stared at him for a beat, not sure I'd heard him correctly. "Did you just say that you're cool with an alien tampering with your brain?"

He shrugged. "Beats the hell out of PTSD. Anyway, I shouldn't be hard to find when you're done cleaning up. Take your time." Ethan patted my shoulder. It hurt.

Rubbing the wall, I nodded while Akata opened a gap for me. The empty chamber inside seemed no different from the clothing one. I stepped inside and watched the wall seal behind me. The walls crowded close and did that massage thing again. When they withdrew, I stood naked in a small room.

Clean, warm water rained from the ceiling, dripping through a hundred tiny holes. I raised my chin to feel the water hitting my face and wondered how I'd ever find makeup out here. Except Ethan and his buddies hadn't commented on how ugly I was, so maybe it didn't matter. As I raised my arms, I wondered how I'd shave anything. Even if they didn't care about that, I did. Dark, stiff hairs on my body bothered me. None of the guys had beards, so I figured they'd found a way.

My period was due...at some point, so I'd have to come up with something for that too. Heck, I didn't even know how to pee here. Thinking about that made me have to go. I noticed the water sluicing away from my feet and saw no better option for the moment. Akata seemed pretty smart, and I guessed she filtered and recycled water already. Otherwise, Ethan would've told me to conserve.

As I straightened from squatting, I thought about toilets. Sometimes, nothing but cool porcelain could calm me down. If space didn't have any, what would I do? Did I need to purge that noodle bowl? Mendez had said it included fat. The enemy. Except I didn't know what else I'd find to eat out here. I knew I needed food to survive, just not as much as I always wound up eating.

Did they have strawberry sauce in space? I wanted it, right now. Except I needed to stay as far away from it as possible. With luck, I'd been flung a bazillion light-years from the nearest source of strawberries. And cheesecake.

My mouth watered. I wanted strawberry cheesecake so hard it hurt. I'd just had some this afternoon. Or whenever that was. Had traveling through that wormhole taken as much time as it had seemed, or did I pop across in a few seconds? I needed a way to get the schematics for the machine so I could figure out how to reverse it.

Water kept falling on my head. I had no idea how to turn it off. Ethan kept saying the ship's name every time he asked for something, so I tried that.

"Akata? I'm done…please?"

The water stopped. Slicking down my hair, I looked up and couldn't see the holes. As I watched, the ceiling surged down and enveloped my head while the walls once again crowded me. This time, the massage warmed me all over. When the room receded, I wore dry clothes on my dry body with dry hair.

This time, I had a blush pink outfit instead of black. Akata listened more than I thought.

Patting my hair, which didn't seem frizzy despite the lack of hair care products, I stepped out of the shower room and tried to decide how I felt about Akata. Everything she did felt both invasive and helpful. Did she have side effects? She kept touching my private parts without making me uncomfortable, unlike every time Andy got into my pants. Did she understand anatomy? Maybe I'd find out the next time I slept with Akata rooting around in my head.

"Read 'em and weep," Nash drawled from the direction of the Mess.

The other guys groaned. When I reached the Mess, I found them sitting around the table. Nash used both hands to drag a small pile of tiny sticks toward himself. Each man had some of what looked like finger bones made of dried blood. I guessed they'd come from Akata. They also had plastic playing cards with faded red ink on the backs and worn edges.

Ethan kicked the extra chair, inviting me to join them. "Do you know how to play poker?"

"More or less," I said as I took the seat. Inspecting a card, I found the usual picture for the queen of hearts.

Mendez chuckled. "That's what a shark says."

"Did you guys bring these with you?" I asked.

"Logan did," Ethan said. He plucked the card out of my hand and added it to the rest of the stack he collected, then he shuffled the deck. "He always carried them around in a pocket."

Nash reached toward me like he wanted to touch my hair. Ethan smacked his hand.

"Just so we're all clear, this is my little sister. She's sixteen. That makes her a minor. And therefore off-limits."

"No, I'm not," I said with a frown. "I'm eighteen."

Ethan squinted at me like I'd spoken Swahili. "No, you're sixteen."

"I think I know how old I am," I grumbled. "I just graduated from high school today. Mom and Dad even showed up for the ceremony." Then they'd patted me on the head and sent me off with my friends with a warning not to drink and drive. Who knew where they went for the evening? Some fancy restaurant, maybe, to celebrate not having to think about me anymore.

Ethan returned to shuffling, his brow still furrowed.

Nash grinned at me. "So she's not off-limits. Because she's an a-dult."

I huffed at him, grossed out by the stuff I thought I saw dancing in his eyes. "She's also sitting right here."

"She's completely off-limits," Ethan growled. "Because she's still my little sister. Keep your hands to yourself."

The room went quiet like Ethan had handed down a directive from God. He dealt the cards and pushed a few sticks toward me. The other three men followed his example and each gave me a handful of sticks. I picked up one and examined it. The tiny shape reminded me more of a bird's bone than my finger.

"What are these?"

"Pieces of blood coral exoskeleton," Mendez said.

"Shells," Baldwin said. He kept his mouth shut a lot, I'd noticed, so I couldn't get an idea of what he sounded like. Maybe he had a bass voice, or maybe he just grunted everything.

"Apparently," Mendez said, "they're used like money on at least one world. That's where we get the food."

I nodded toward Ethan. "He said none of the aliens

have been friendly."

"I wouldn't call the greenies friendly," Nash said. "More like willing to trade for something they want."

"Greenies?"

Mendez shrugged. "They're green. No idea what they call themselves. We just point to the stuff we want and hand over the shells."

"Language has been a real problem out here," Ethan said. He set the cards aside and picked up his hand. With the change of topic, he seemed to have mellowed again. "But we do a little more than grunt and point with the greenies now. We've learned some of the names for things and the basic number words."

"For the greenies," Nash said. "Not for anybody else. There's no trade language. At least, none we've run across. You'd think they'd come up with one in a part of space where a bunch of different races mix, but you'd be wrong."

"There's some kind of translating gizmo," Ethan said, "but we can't figure out how to get one."

A device to translate languages sounded like the first thing I'd want to buy, steal, or build in a situation like this. Eating mattered, sure, but talking to everyone seemed important too. These guys seemed to have given up on the idea of communicating. Maybe they'd been out here too long to care.

I picked up my cards and arranged them in descending order. Queen high and nothing else in my five cards—not even three parts of a straight. "Who dealt this crap?"

Ethan smirked at me and pushed my one-stick ante into the center of the table with the other four sticks already there. "I think you're right, Mendez. She's probably a shark."

"When the stakes are high, you learn the rules fast," I muttered.

"What kind of stakes would those be?" Ethan asked.

Baldwin opened the betting round with one stick.

Everyone matched. No one raised. I dropped three cards to get new ones.

I wanted to ignore the question and pretend like I hadn't heard him. After a long pause, Ethan cleared his throat. He drummed his fingers on the table.

Fine. if he wanted to ask questions like that, then I'd answer them. "Stripping."

Ethan stilled and stared at me for a beat. "Excuse me?"

"You bet pieces of clothing—"

"I know what strip poker is."

"Then why did you ask?"

Narrowing his eyes, he pushed three new cards at me. "How do *you* know what strip poker is?"

My new cards gave me a pair of fours. Considering Mendez had only traded one card and Ethan two, I didn't think I had a chance. I didn't know these guys well enough to bluff, either. Setting my cards down, I shrugged at Ethan.

"Probably the same reason you do."

"Zing," Mendez said with a chuckle.

Ethan raised his brow. "I played my first round at a bar near Pendleton with some other recruits and a handful of hookers trying to fleece us. They let us in because we had military ID and a Corporal who vouched for us because he wanted to get drunk."

Nash and Mendez both laughed. Baldwin smirked. I blushed. Ethan hadn't written about that in any of his letters home.

I cleared my throat and tried to play it cool. "Then I guess it wasn't exactly the same. None of us were hookers."

"How old were you?" His gaze bored into me, like he expected to find the answer etched into my skull. "How much did you drink?"

His questions made me remember that night. I didn't want to remember that night. It had all started with giggling, but it hadn't ended that way.

"Aw, who cares," Nash said, startling me out of the

memory. "You in or out?"

Ethan scowled at his cards and smacked them on the table. He stood and stalked out.

I let him go because I didn't know what to say.

CHAPTER 8

Mendez leaned close and lowered his voice. "Don't be too hard on him. He's been in command almost since we got here, and he takes it really serious. There's four of us left, and he still acts like everything is his responsibility." He patted my arm.

I nodded, though I didn't know what to make of that. Did Mendez mean that Ethan needed a vacation? "Is this all you guys do for fun? Play cards?"

"This and exercise," Nash said. "Not much else to do. We didn't get new information to go on for the next raid on the transmission station, so we gotta come up some new idea, but that ain't gonna happen by banging our heads against a wall. Gotta stand down and make sure we're healed up before we think about another run."

None of the men sported bandages or seemed injured, so I didn't know what he meant about healing. Regardless, I didn't know all the information they already had. To help, I needed to know as much as possible. Learning about the situation would distract me from everything else, which I considered a value-added bonus.

"What's the deal with the sentinels? Are they inside the station or surrounding it, or what?"

Baldwin dropped his cards and propped his feet on the table. "Outside."

"The sentinels shoot concussive blasts," Mendez said. "They're outside, but they shoot at the station while we're inside. The blast doesn't harm electronics, but it moves stuff and scrambles brains. I don't know if you noticed the way the station rocked when you first woke up out here?" When I nodded, he continued. "That was the sentinels. There are parts of the station they can reach to target us specifically and parts they can't."

"Akata, make the table into a station map," Nash said.

With a tiny huff, Baldwin removed his feet. The table's surface rippled and peeled away to reveal a screen. On the screen, the clear, sharp picture showed the transmission station I'd seen before. Instead of remaining flat, something projected the image above the table. The holographic view zoomed in until it showed a three dimensional schematic of the station. Outer layers separated to let me see inner layers, and a red line ran through it, creating a path from the outside to a spot near the center.

I poked the outer shell of the station with my finger and felt resistance, as if I'd touched an actual object. With a few more nudges, I discovered I could manipulate the model to see what I wanted. Layers expanded or contracted as I plucked or pushed them, and I could turn the model to change my view. This made CAD software seem pathetic.

"This is so cool," I breathed.

"I guess so," Mendez said with an amused smile. "The red line is the most direct path we've found. Blank parts are bits we haven't explored, so Akata has no data to fill in."

"Where are the turbines?" I asked as I kept prodding the model.

Nash, Mendez, and Baldwin glanced at each other. I saw a twinkle of something in their eyes—hope, maybe.

"What you see is what we know about," Mendez said. "If it's not on there, we haven't seen it or Akata couldn't figure out what it was from what we did see."

"Would any of you know a turbine if you saw one?"

"Maybe," Baldwin said with a shrug.

Nash nodded. "Only if it looked like something I seen before."

"We're grunts," Mendez said, "not tech guys. We carry rifles, storm beaches, and handle explosives. That's our training."

"I don't know how to do any of those things." I rotated the model and wanted more information about the facility. The biggest design I'd concocted so far had been a colonizing ship for Mars, and I knew it needed work. Tech hadn't advanced enough for the directions I wanted to take it. My model of a different design, still lying unfinished on my desk at home, also needed tech humans hadn't discovered yet. "Is there anyone on the facility? Living creatures, I mean."

"Not that we can tell. Everything seems automated. No sign of anyone at all."

Still playing with the model, I pointed to a dark spot with no detail. "How impossible would it be to scout these blank areas?"

Mendez shrugged. "We can last about ten minutes against the robots trying to mess with us. That's typically when our rifles run out of power."

"Our weapons," Nash said, "the ones the robots gave us, use energy packs. Akata can recharge them. Each pack takes an hour or so."

"They don't destroy the robots, though," Mendez said. "Porter knocked one offline using his gun from Earth, but there's no ammo out here and no way to make our own. Likewise, we managed to cause some real damage with a grenade once, but we've only got so many grenades. The facility repairs and replaces robots, so that's pointless until we know we're going home without a doubt."

I poked the model, causing its layers to telescope in and out. If I wanted to design something like this, I'd cluster the biggest power drains around the engines and the most critical systems with a buffer in case of explosion. Basic, automated security would have multiple access points for redundancy.

"What we need to do," I said, not thinking about how to accomplish it, "is disable the station without destroying the power grid. That way, we'll be able to scout for as long as we want. Depending on how it works, I might be able to rig it in reverse during the power outage, then we can bring the juice back up and hop through to go home."

Nash smirked. "Sure, we'll just mosey in and cut off the power. No problem."

"Lay off." Mendez nudged Nash in the side. "She just got here and she's already working on how to get us home. That's better than any of us did on our first day."

My cheeks burned. "I didn't mean it would be easy or anything. I just don't see how I can get enough information to do my part in ten minutes."

"Scouting," Baldwin said. "Harper won't like it."

"He doesn't like anything except success," Mendez said with a snort.

That didn't sound like Ethan to me. My big brother had always been my shelter, not my taskmaster. When I got lousy grades, he'd helped me figure out how to fix that without griping about how horrible I'd done. Dad did the griping and yelling.

I shook my head. Thinking about the past didn't help. "Have you scouted the facility before? I mean, just pure scouting."

The three men looked to each other. After a few seconds of what looked like telepathic communication, they shook their heads.

"We never go in without an objective of finding that wormhole machine thing," Nash said.

"I think it might be worthwhile," I said.

Mendez tapped under my chin with a finger. "No, chica. Say 'we need to do this.' Feel it. Mean it. That's how you convince him."

He wanted me to hold my head high and believe I knew what to do and how to do it. I didn't. All of us could die. More than anything, I wanted to hang out in Akata with Ethan and never go home. I stopped fussing with the model and dropped my gaze to the floor.

"What if I'm wrong?"

"What if you're right?" Nash asked.

"I don't want to get anyone killed on a maybe."

"Suck it up, princess," Baldwin said. He'd finally uttered enough words for me to hear his Boston lilt.

Mendez waved him off. "The first time I saw someone die, it was over a willow tree. Trunk on one side of a property line, branches on the other. Two grown men argued about that damned tree every summer for five years. The last time they argued about it, one had a chainsaw. He cut off a branch and it hit the other on the head, cracking his skull open."

I stared at him in horror. And had no idea why he told that story.

"That's pointless death," Mendez said. "Stupid, worthless, pointless death. This? Struggling to get out of here and back home? I'd die for that. If my death meant the rest of you get back to Earth, then that's fine with me. Let's do it." He grinned. "I'd rather not, of course. Nobody shoot me to make it come true."

Baldwin and Nash snickered at him. I kept staring. They saw humor in death. Did facing it often do that to a person? Would it happen to me? I didn't want it to.

Mendez tapped the tip of my nose. "Ah, chica, you're precious. Don't ever change."

Flinching from Mendez, I wondered if I could find a corner of the ship to escape these guys without going insane from loneliness or boredom. Maybe they needed more things to do. I knew I did. Something else to do would save me from having to sit here and try to understand soldiers.

"We need a plan," Nash said. "Something Harper ain't gonna shoot down in five seconds."

"What, you don't think 'walk in and do some stuff' will fly?" Mendez said with a wink.

Baldwin laughed. "No."

I shrugged and picked up a piece of coral money. The coral had a brain controlling it for the ship, but did that mean it needed a brain? "Can we take some of the live coral and use it handheld? Like, can it operate independently of the brain? Or from a distance?"

All three men stared at me. That thing flickered in their eyes again. Yep, definitely hope.

Had Ethan ever noticed their despair? Probably not, especially if he suffered from it too.

Someone needed to give him shoulder to lean on. By which I meant me.

CHAPTER 9

"Hey, Ethan?" I found him in the only other room with a vein sign. They had weights made from mismatched metal pieces and a giant hamster wheel of blood coral. Entering the room felt like too much intrusion, so I stayed at the open gap, leaning against the wall.

Ethan sat on a bench, lifting and lowering a ragged hunk of metal with a handle attached to one side. I imagined he did that a lot. "It's funny how weird it is to have someone use my first name."

I thought that sounded like a routine hazard of military life. "Did you have a girlfriend back home?" The idea of "back home" meaning "planet Earth" both amused and depressed me.

"Give me a little credit. I would've mentioned it in a letter if I had someone serious. Do you have a boyfriend?"

"No." Unless Andy counted. "Sort of." I crossed my arms so I wouldn't squirm on the outside. "Not really."

"Did you go to prom with him?"

"We all went as a group." Madison and Andy had ridden in my car. I'd picked them up and dropped them off, so Mom and Dad never got pictures of anyone except me.

I hadn't stopped in to talk about dating or prom. Him bringing it up made me want to, but we had more important things to worry about. Remembering what Mendez had said, I raised my chin and tried to exude confidence. "Anyway, I want to scout the transmission facility."

He stopped, set down the weight, and straightened to look at me. "Scout it?"

"Yeah. Knock out the power temporarily and map the place, maybe do some on-the-fly rewiring if I can. Taking something with circuitry would be helpful so I can see how it all works. Then we can make a plan to actually use the facility to get home."

For a few beats, he stared at me like I'd spoken a foreign language. "And how do you propose we knock out the power temporarily?"

I gulped and blushed. Did he need a guarantee before agreeing? I didn't know. "I have no idea? I've been inside it once, and I wasn't conscious the whole time."

"And that makes this plan seem feasible how?"

"It's not a plan, it's an idea. I don't have enough information to make a plan. Plans is your department unless it's a ship plan, in which case I'll handle it."

He stared again. I thought I might've pissed him off, or stepped too far beyond . Then he cracked a faint grin. "Right." As he stood, he seemed to collect himself, though I hadn't noticed anything scattered about him. "Two objectives, then. One is to get a piece of the facility you can use to understand how it's wired. The other is to find and disable the power system for a more thorough investigation of the rest of the systems."

Though he hadn't made any of those statements sound like a question, I nodded anyway. "Yes."

"Would a robot drone be enough to understand how the station works? We could grab one of those without too much trouble."

I frowned and thought about it. "If the station designer also designed the robots, then yes. Taking apart a robot would help me figure out if I can even do anything to the wormhole system. If they had different designers, it could help or it could be worthless."

"But we don't know that and have no way to find out." Ethan crossed his arms and drummed his fingers on his bicep. He had huge muscles. From lifting weights with all his free time, I guessed. These guys really needed more things to do besides cards and brooding. "And when we grab a piece of the station, we can't take anything critical because we want to use the wormhole device."

Though I hadn't thought of that tiny problem, I decided to believe I would have before we got there. "Something on one of the ends would probably work." I thought of the holographic diagram and considered all the parts. "Or one of the spinning rings. Does Akata have any weapons?"

"Not that we've seen."

Considering their brain interfacing, I suspected Akata had no such capability. She would've seen interest in weapons from a bunch of soldiers and produced them. Unless they hadn't had the ship long, except they seemed to have settled into a routine with her.

"How did you wind up with Akata, anyway?"

"Accident." Ethan beckoned for me to follow as he left the room. "She was locked in a container on the first ship we assaulted. We needed an escape option."

That first ship must've been enormous. With what I could guess of Akata's size, the idea of a dozen Marines assaulting something big enough to hold her in a container boggled my mind.

"So you've been traveling on this ship for about two years?"

"Yeah. That was a few days after we got here." He took me back to the Mess, where the other three men had resumed playing cards. "Does that matter?"

"Not really." For two years, these guys had let Akata root through their thoughts and memories. In all that time, not one of them had used her insights to come up with a better strategy than storming the facility to reach the wormhole device and hope they could somehow figure out how to use it.

He took his seat again, so I followed suit. "Emma needs a piece of the facility. Thoughts about how to get one for her? Discount the robots, which would be too much trouble anyway."

Nash shrugged. "Walk in, rip up some stuff, take some of it, walk out."

"Maybe we can take it from the outside," Mendez said. "Like, cozy up next to the end and cut some parts off."

"Cut? With karate chop action?" Nash asked.

"Crowbar?" Baldwin asked.

Ethan shook his head. "There's breathable air inside, and we need to keep it that way. So we're going inside. But we can probably get something from the area around the airlock."

"What if we mess up the airlock?" Nash asked. "We ain't got space suits, and Akata can only protect us a few feet away from the ship."

That explained how we'd hopped across a gap in space to get from the facility to the ship. "Is there anything preventing Akata from touching the facility? You said it repairs itself, so we only have to worry about what happens while we're there. If Akata can effectively shield us from any problem with the airlock by covering the hole, there's no issue."

Mendez nodded. "She's smarter than you, Harper."

Ethan rolled his eyes. "Of course she is. But she's not coming into the facility with us." He looked at me. "At least, not this time."

I opened my mouth to protest, but stopped. Like I'd said before, I didn't know how to use a rifle or smash things. Maybe I needed to fix that, but risking all of our lives to bring me sounded stupid when I just wanted parts to study. "Okay. I get that. I'll stay behind while you all go do the Marines thing. I need intact electronics. If you can grab three or four different kinds of stuff, that'd be best."

They all nodded. Mendez took the cards to shuffle.

"Akata," Ethan said, "we're going back to the facility."

"Now?" I stared at the other three men. They seemed fine with the order. "We're going back right now?"

"Is there a reason to wait?" Ethan asked.

"I don't know? Nash said you need to heal up and rest or something."

"We're fine," Baldwin said.

Marines. I didn't know what to think about them anymore. These guys had weird ideas about everything.

"Sure. You're fine. Okay. What should I do while you storm the barricades? And how long until we get there?"

The table covering peeled apart again. This time, no one expected it. Coral sticks and cards flew off the surface and landed everywhere, including my lap, to a chorus of surprised grunts and annoyed groans. The screen projected a clock. It counted backward from 1:13:23, which, based upon the speed of the final number, seemed to mean one hour and thirteen minutes.

"Thank you, Akata," Ethan said with an exasperated sigh. "You stay out of the way. That's your job."

I pressed my mouth shut, not sure what I could offer.

"She could stand by the door," Mendez said as he crouched to pick up coral pieces. "We can bring her stuff and she can tell us if it's useful or not. Keep track of who's on the ship and who's not."

"Yeah," Nash said. He gathered the cards. "If we give her extra rifles, we can trade them out instead of giving up when the first packs run out of juice."

Though I didn't want to negate a reason for me to do something, I didn't understand this problem. "Why don't you just leave them by the door?"

Ethan shook his head. "We've tried that. Exposure to the field around the ship depletes the charges. It's fine for the amount of time it takes us to hop across the gap, but not much longer."

"There's a field around the ship?" I wanted a space suit so I could check it out. Or a portable camera. Maybe I only needed to interface with Akata. She probably knew everything about the ship. We had a plan, though, and the Marines had decided to go full speed ahead.

"Yeah. You can kinda see it if you squint while looking from the outside," Mendez said.

"Oh." Lucky me, I got to stay on the ship while they all left. "If I'm just inside the ship, though, how will that change anything for the rifles? Won't they lose charge anyway? Why can't you just carry two?"

All four men stared like I'd asked if they'd please wear tutus for me.

"It's not feasible to carry two rifles and still do things," Mendez said after a long silence. "You could hold one deep enough in the ship for it to not matter, bring it to the airlock when we call, then fetch another one and hold that."

They wanted me to pass things back and forth. Instead of doing something active, I'd stand near the door and wait. I couldn't decide if that bothered me or not. Logistically, it made a lot of sense. This whole crazy space thing, though, seemed like an awful lot of boredom. If even their missions would bore me to tears, I didn't know how long I'd manage before I cracked.

"Okay." Did I have any other options besides agreeing? Not really. Until I came up with a viable way to assist, I needed to avoid causing problems. And here I'd thought being stuck with my brother and his Marine buddies would be better than going home.

I tried not to show my disappointment. "I guess that sounds like a plan."

CHAPTER 10

White veins showed a circle with two X's for eyes, marking the invisible seam that would open to let the guys out of the ship. We waited beside it, though I stood twenty feet deeper in the ship than any of them. The four men wore black vests covered in bulging pockets, and each carried a rifle. Ethan had a crowbar hanging from a belt loop.

I had a rifle too. Even if I wanted to, I couldn't have carried two at once. My arms could barely lift the one. While we waited, I saved myself from fatigue by leaving the butt end resting on the floor. When it came time to pass one over, I didn't know if they'd regret relying on me or not. Right now, I felt like an over-glorified umbrella stand.

So far, I hadn't noticed any sensations while Akata flew. She hadn't turned in any way that I could tell, though we must've reversed course somehow. Even if we'd decelerated and moved in the opposite direction without turning, I thought I should've noticed. Nope. For all I knew, the ship stayed still while the universe moved around it.

As soon as I wondered how we'd know if the ship stopped, my world rolled sideways. I felt like my mind shifted two feet to the left while my body twisted to the right. The bottom fell out of my stomach. My vision crowded with static. I wondered if this meant I'd dreamed about finding Ethan and now I went to the real Hell.

All the sensations faded with me still standing behind four Marines, still holding up an enormous rifle, still waiting. For the first time in a long time, I felt like throwing up but didn't want to. I remembered feeling that way the last time I had the flu, in fifth grade.

"Ugh." I covered my mouth and leaned against the wall.

"Yeah, stopping is kind of crappy," Mendez said. He reached over and rubbed my arm. "You get used to it."

"I hope not," I muttered.

"Get ready," Ethan said. This seemed to mean that I should shut up.

Mendez flashed me a sympathetic smile. I returned it. The vein symbol changed the X's to O's. The floor and wall quivered with a mild impact. Baldwin, standing ready to rush in first, touched the wall over the symbol. The wall split apart, creating a gap wide enough for the guys to charge through.

Through the gap, black metal blocked passage. No one seemed surprised. Baldwin bent and did something. The black metal parted along multiple seams, like a camera iris opening. Baldwin slipped through. Ethan followed with Nash next and Mendez in the rear.

As he stepped across to the station, Mendez turned back and saluted me. I nodded and watched him disappear into the red-tinted gloom.

And then I waited.

My head resting against the wall, I considered stepping across the gap and into the facility. I could take a look at the construction. Knowing how the facility had been put together might help me figure out how to get at the power supply or conduits. They'd said the rifles tended to last about ten minutes, so if I kept my visit brief, no one would know.

I leaned the rifle against the wall in my stead. For some reason, I glanced around to check if anyone saw me. Then I tiptoed to the hole in the wall and ducked my head across. Light pressure shimmered across my head and neck.

The pushing on my neck made me uncomfortable, so I stepped through.

Metal grating covered the floor, and sheet metal made up the walls and ceiling. I squatted to run my hand over the floor. Orderly rectangular slits about the width of my finger covered the floor plates. Inside the slits, a wire grid criss-crossed the gaps.

I poked the grid.

Mistake.

Electric current jolted my body. My teeth chattered. I jerked my finger away. The stupid plate had grounded me because my finger touched it at the same time as the wire. At least I'd learned something. Whether it wound up helping anything was another matter.

Rubbing my temples against a headache, I crawled back to the ship. The guys had been right. I didn't belong in the facility. They did action and plans. I did ideas. Stupid ideas, probably. When the guys returned, I'd find out for sure, but I had a feeling nothing would come of this.

How did I think getting a piece of the facility would help anything? It wouldn't tell me about the arrangement of the systems or how to shut down the power grid. I didn't even understand why the facility existed. Who had built it? Why did it have gravity and air? How did they get a vision into all of our heads of cyborg wolfmen, and why?

I sat beside the rifle, hugging my knees and feeling useless. Of all the people Ethan could've brought across, why me? He could've snared a real engineer. If he'd gotten Dad, he would've had a genuine accountant, someone who'd graduated from college and had all kinds of knowledge that probably would've been more helpful. And Dad knew how to shoot a gun. He'd learned from Grandpa, who'd been a Marine once upon a time.

But no, they got worthless me. I wanted a toilet to purge into, except I hadn't eaten anything but noodle bowl in hours. By this point, I'd digested enough to make purging pointless. Throwing up bile sucked. Not knowing how to get a glass of water made everything worse.

"Hey, chica, are you okay?"

Lifting my head, I saw Mendez. He dropped a thin, jagged piece of something gray beside me. Lines of dark ink or plastic, or something, snaked across the plate.

"Yeah. Just bored."

"Now you have something to do." He flashed me a smile oozing with confidence and hurried back into the facility.

I wanted to feel that certain about something. Trying not to feel guilty about lying to Mendez, I sighed. He hadn't really wanted to know, after all. People never wanted to know. They asked to make conversation.

Picking up the plate, I shrugged off the crap in my head. I wanted to, anyway. Inspecting the plate helped. The smooth, gray material had a texture between metal and plastic. My fingernails clicked when I tapped it. Each thin, dark line had a tiny ridge in the center, and they felt rubbery, like the clear stuff plumbers used to seal around sinks. Checking it from the edge, I noticed the ridge had been created by a light-colored cylinder surrounded by the dark stuff.

"Rifle!"

Startled, I snapped up my head and saw Ethan charging toward me. I scrambled to my feet, yanked the rifle off the wall, and hauled it as far as I could. The butt end dragged on the floor, filling the air with horrible screeching.

Ethan dropped his rifle with a clatter as he reached me and snatched the fresh one out of my hands. He lifted it as if it weighed nothing. As suddenly as he appeared, he disappeared again into the relative darkness of the facility.

My job sent me running deeper into the ship to fetch another rifle. I hauled it thirty feet, from the secure stash to the waiting spot. Why couldn't they have set up all the rifles at the waiting spot? I'd only gotten the same vague half-answers as before about losing charge near the airlock. Something about that seemed fishy to me. Yet again, I wished we'd waited until after I got to interface with Akata.

Of course, I had no idea why that hadn't happened before. I'd been in a pod when I woke up. Maybe I'd been unconscious instead of asleep, and maybe that mattered.

Mendez returned with another piece of the facility, this one a gray box with dark lines across one side. He flashed me a smile as he tossed it to me.

I flinched. The box hit my thigh and fell into my lap. My fat jiggled, and it hurt. Mendez already had his back turned when I looked up. Thank goodness, or he would've seen how gross I was.

My attention turned to the box. The gray material and dark lines seemed the same as the plate. Picking it up, I noticed the box had seams on only one side. One piece of the material had been formed as a cube with a flap to enclose it. Unlike a normal metal box, though, the seams hadn't been welded shut. Instead, they'd been sealed with some kind of opalescent stuff. When I touched it, the stuff wiggled like my thighs.

Nash interrupted my inspection with a demand for another rifle. I helped him swap as much as I could. By the time I returned with the third replacement rifle, Ethan showed up, needing it. Whatever he did in the facility involved a lot of shooting, apparently.

As he plunged into the facility again, I heard a deep thrumming noise. The facility's airlock shifted to the left. Akata rolled to match it. My two specimens of alien tech slid toward the facility as if trying to escape. I scrambled after them. Near the gap, I heard shouting without making out the words. Boots clomped on metal at high speed, approaching me.

The foray was about to end, I gathered. Scooping up my new treasures, I scuttled deeper into Akata to get out of the guys' way. Ethan charged across the gap first. Nash and

Baldwin following him, carrying Mendez's limp body between them.

"Oh my God! Is he okay?" I lurched toward him, wanting to help.

Ethan caught me before I could rush to Mendez. He wrapped his arm around my and held me close. "Akata, get us out of here!"

As before, static clouded my vision and my stomach roiled. My body seemed distant and weird.

CHAPTER 11

"What's wrong with you?" Ethan held me against his chest with one thick arm while I recovered from whatever Akata did.

"Nothing. What about Mendez?" I checked behind him and saw nothing but the closed seam in Akata's outer wall.

"He's fine. Just knocked out. The robots have something like a taser they use." Ethan let go and helped me settle on me feet. His arm still around my shoulder, he touched my cheek and pulled down my lower eyelid. He peered into my eyes with a frown. "People who have nothing wrong don't sway on their feet and fail to respond."

"You mean you don't feel nauseous or anything?" My belly quieted, but I wanted to run under the shower again. My skin itched with grime. I had no idea why.

"No." He kissed my forehead and shifted his grip so we stood side-by-side. At his urging, we walked deeper into the ship. "Does anything else happen when Akata folds space?"

"Folds space? What does that even mean?"

"That's what she calls it. We move through space really fast, basically. You'd probably understand it better than me."

Folding space sounded fascinating. I wanted to know how it worked. Taking a step while I considered the possibilities, I tripped over nothing and almost fell. If not for

Ethan's grip on my shoulders, I would've faceplanted.

He stopped and frowned at me. His concern radiated in waves, lapping against me with a sharp yet gentle edge. "I think you should eat something."

"Ugh. No, thanks."

"Rest, then."

"I'll interface with Akata when I sleep, won't I? And she'll answer questions?" When he nodded, I held up the plate and box. "I want to look at these first."

We passed the sleeping room, where Baldwin and Nash worked on settling Mendez into a pod. Ethan steered me into the Mess and pushed me into a chair. I sat and set my two treasures on the table. Running my fingers over the plate, I wondered how to pry open the box.

"Do you still have that crowbar?" I asked.

"Mendez had it last. He probably dropped it."

I poked the seam on the box. The goo squished without vacating the seam or sticking to my finger. "You're sure he'll be okay?"

"Yeah. If he has a concussion, Akata'll take care of him. I'm more worried about you."

Eager to talk about anything other than me, I latched onto Akata's apparently bottomless well of capability. "You kind of rely on Akata for a lot."

Ethan shrugged. "Not like we have a ton of options out here."

Nothing about that statement invited argument. Obviously, they couldn't go to a hospital or an emergency room. Even if they could, the doctors probably knew nothing about human anatomy.

With that thought, I remembered again that Ethan and the others had been out here for two years. In all that time, they hadn't found any other human beings. They'd watched their friends die, one by one. They all expected to die out here, trying and failing to get home. Someone, they must have realized, would wind up as the last man standing.

And into this group, accident had dropped me onto my butt. Our fates all depended upon me figuring out the facility and reversing that wormhole generating device. The odds seemed crappy. I knew a lot, but I hadn't actually built anything more complex than a potato-powered clock. Everything else had been theoretical.

For some reason, building spaceships and rockets required materials a girl in high school had no access to. Go figure.

I prodded the two dark lines on the side of the box. They ran from an edge with a seam halfway across the side, and then stopped. At the edge, it had been chopped, probably with the end of the crowbar. At the halfway point, though, the end seemed smooth and rounded. Intentional. Why end the line there?

The stupid box held secrets, and I wanted them.

"Do you have any ideas about prying this open?" I held up the box for Ethan.

He whipped out a knife. I had no idea where he kept it, because I hadn't noticed a sheath strapped to any part of his person. The black-handled knife had a six inch blade of dull red material, probably made of blood coral exoskeleton.

When he tapped the table, I set down the box. He laid the sharp edge on a seam and pressed. The goo squished under his firm assault. Not until his arm muscles bulged did the point shove through.

Sawing through the goo seemed to take an impressive amount of effort. He clenched his jaw. Sweat beaded on his forehead. As he reached the corner, he growled at it.

"What *is* this stuff? It's harder to cut through than a bone."

I decided I didn't want to know if he had experience with that. "Glue?"

"Or something." He pried the seam open enough to wedge the knife around the corner and kept going.

"What's that?" Nash strolled into the room.

Baldwin followed him. As he passed me to take a seat, he lobbed something at the table. A small, square piece of the gray material hit the red-brown surface with a soft thump.

I picked up the new piece of the facility. Lying flat, it covered my open hand from my wrist to the end of my middle finger. One black line ran from an edge to the center. Like the box, the ends at both edges had been sawed off.

Flipping it over, I found a one-inch metal bar with two more black lines leading to the opposite edge. The arrangement gave me suspicions, because the metal bar touched one black line but not the other. I grasped the bar and twisted it. When it flipped to the other black line with a click, I knew what I had in my hand.

"A toggle switch," I murmured. That meant the black lines transmitted power.

"What?"

I didn't notice which man asked because questions whirled in my head too fast to care. If the black lines worked like wires, why did the floor have metal wires? How did the material conduct electricity? How did the facility generate power? The place had to use a lot, even when the wormhole device wasn't active.

Ethan grunted and set the box in front of me, the flap cut loose of the goo. I picked it up and tried to pry the flap open. When I couldn't, Nash took it and bent the gray material as easily as cardboard.

Inside, I found a collection of three tiny fan blades made of the gray material. The black lines that I had thought ended halfway across the box's side actually ended inside a hole. Copper wires plunged into the center of each.

Three tiny fans closed inside a box made no sense, but I didn't care. Now I knew how all this stuff worked, more or less. They'd used unfamiliar materials with familiar principles. Knowing that, I thought I could figure out how to reverse the wormhole, provided hardware controlled it. If software determined that, we had no hope of reprogramming it.

"Do we have any potatoes?"

When no one answered me, I looked up to see all three men staring like I'd grown an extra head. These guys didn't seem interested or excited, and I couldn't imagine why not. Understanding this stuff meant I could probably disable the robots and security systems in the facility, which would give us plenty of time to find the control systems.

With another moment of thought, though, the potato request sounded stupid.

"Right. Alien food means alien plants. Sorry. I need something that generates electricity."

Ethan shrugged. "There are no outlets in the walls, if that's what you mean. Maybe you should ask Akata when you interface. She might have some ideas for how to do what you want."

"Okay. How about tools? Do we have any?"

Nash made a fist and thumped it on the table with a grin. "We got hammers."

Something else to ask Akata about, I gathered, because they'd never thought to get a screwdriver. Then again, screwdrivers might not help. Considering the goo on the box, I needed something to deactivate or dissolve it more than anything else. I couldn't just cart one of these guys around to cut into whatever I needed. Even if I could, cutting the outside could cut the inside. Something important could be destroyed by accident, and I had no way to repair it.

"Can you get these little fans out for me?" I pushed the box at Ethan.

He stuck his hand inside and wiggled it. After a few moments, he withdrew it. "Probably not without breaking something."

The fans moved, which meant they hadn't been grown or molded there, so I knew they could be removed. I wanted to see what they'd been mounted on. Sticking my own hand in, I wriggled until I could see under my palm and slipped a fingernail under the cap in the center.

"What do you figure this stuff is?" Nash tapped the big plate with a fingertip.

"Who knows," Ethan said with a shrug. "Who cares?"

"I kind of care," I said. "But really, I only care if it's conductive or not, and how it interacts with water."

My fingernail broke. The stupid cap had been wedged too hard for me to remove. Now I needed a screwdriver. Ethan's knife would probably cut through the fan, and I didn't want that. The idea of a tiny crowbar made me grin.

I inspected my fingernail and chewed on the ragged edge, thinking about all the questions I needed to ask Akata.

Weariness couldn't come soon enough.

CHAPTER 12

We played cards for a while. No one had much to say. When Ethan got up to spend some time lifting weights, I followed him. Exercise would help me fall asleep.

As I settled on a bench with my back to his and a two-pound weight in each hand, I wondered about that thought. If exercise tended to help me sleep—which it did—the possibility existed that I'd fallen asleep before taking my shower. All this could still be Hell, but it could also be a weird dream.

I imagined myself lying on the floor, covered with grime. At some point, Mom or Dad would come looking for me. No, on second thought, I'd wake up before that ever happened. If they called out and I didn't answer, they'd assume I'd gone out. Even with my car in the garage.

Except the boredom felt real. When I dreamed, I always had cream puffs with strawberry sauce attacking, or mirrors exploding, or other things going on. Never once had I dreamed about having nothing to do and wanting time to pass faster. That only happened in real life. Probably, that also happened in Hell.

"Are you sure we're not dead?"

Ethan paused in his curls. "What?"

"What if we're all dead and this is Hell?"

He resumed his lifting. After another minute of

silence, during which I pondered the question more, he asked, "Why do you think you'd go to Hell when you die?"

I shrugged. "This is definitely not Heaven."

"I'm pretty sure I'm not dead, so you aren't either. You might not last long if you don't put some meat on your bones, though. You're practically a walking pile of sticks."

"I'm not." I'd never understood boys. They saw the whole world through some bizarre lens that denied reality.

"You are. I'm worried I'll snap you in half if I look at you too hard."

"Whatever." If I had anything better to do, I would've left to do it.

Ethan stopped again and turned. He patted my shoulder. When I looked, I saw him frowning with concern. "You're really skinny, Cog. I can see your ribs and the bones in your shoulders. That's not right." He wrapped his hand around my wrist and lifted it. "How can you not see this?"

I saw the flab dangling from my upper arm and grimaced. "I know I'm a freak, okay? You don't have to tell me."

"Freak? You're not a freak." He let go and brushed hair behind my ear. "You remind me of some kids I saw once in the Sandbox. Gaunt and weak because they were on that ragged edge of eating almost enough all the time, instead of true starvation. Lieutenant told us not to give them any food because it wouldn't solve anything. They'd get a blast of nutrition that would make them worse off when they couldn't keep it up, and we'd be out a meal."

"You're nuts." I turned away from him and dropped the weights. They thumped on the floor. "I'm not hungry."

My stomach growled. We'd spent too much time talking about food.

He caught my arm. It hurt. "Why do you keep saying that when you definitely are?"

"I'm fine," I snapped. Standing, I tried to yank my arm out of his grip, but had no chance. "Let go."

"No. Not until you talk to me about this."

"About what?" I kept trying to wriggle free, but he wouldn't let go. My eyes itched, warning me I could expect tears to fall any minute.

He stood, making me feel like a dwarf. "What's been going on at home? Did Mom or Dad lose their jobs? Are they having financial problems?"

"What does that have to do with anything?" I tugged harder, wanting to be anyplace else.

"I'm trying to understand why you haven't been eating enough for so long that you look like this."

Tears rushed in. "Thanks for pointing out how ugly I am. Like I can't see that every time I look in a mirror."

"Stop squirming." Jerking me close, he wrapped an arm around my waist. With that move, he rendered escape impossible. "Calm down."

I sagged and covered my face, wishing I didn't feel anything. Ethan lowered me to the floor and rubbed my back while I cried. He made shushing and soothing noises. At least when my tears subsided, I only felt tired.

"What's going on with you, Cog?"

"I don't know." I wiped my nose on my sleeve.

He hugged me close without forcing me to look at him. "Who hurt you?"

How could I tell him the truth? I couldn't. The truth hurt even more than the problem. "Nobody."

"I don't believe you."

"I don't care." I didn't mean that, but I didn't take it back.

With a heavy sighed, he loosened his grip. "Me. Was it me?"

I stared at the floor. Yes. No. Also yes. And also no.

"I'll take that as a yes." He left a few beats of quiet. I didn't fill them. "We both knew I was going to enlist, Cog. For a long time."

For years, he'd been hell-bent on joining the Air Force.

71

The fastest track into the astronaut program required piloting experience. He'd wanted that so hard.

"You were going to go to college first. You were going to take pilot lessons."

"I was going to do a lot of things." He helped me sit, leaning against him. "I never told you about what happened to make me change my mind."

Crossing my arms, I wished he'd stop talking and let me go. I could lie in that stupid pod, waiting for sleep. That sounded better than picking at scabs and scars. "No, you didn't. You just brought home a brochure for the Marines two weeks before you graduated and had a shouting match with Dad about the Accounting program at Bentley. Which he signed me up for, by the way."

"I wouldn't call it a shouting match."

"But it was one. I could hear you from inside my bedroom."

Ethan huffed. He sounded amused. "Fine, it was a shouting match. But I was never going to go to Bentley, no matter how much he wanted me to. And you shouldn't either."

"I figured I could fail out and convince him to let me go someplace else."

"That's a crappy plan."

I shrugged. My brain had stalled the day Dad had told me about Bentley. Picking at my fingernails, I remembered trying to summon the nerve to resist like Ethan had. I'd failed. Meek and weak, Freaky McFreakingfreak had wilted like leaves in jet exhaust. I'd never been able to resist Andy either.

Thinking back over the past few years, I remembered wanting to shout at Bridget but never doing it. I remembered wanting to refuse Tiffany something but failing to say it. I remembered wanting to shove my knee between Andy's legs but balking at the pain I knew he'd feel.

Every time, they got what they wanted, and I got nothing or worse. They taunted me and I stayed quiet. When they'd laughed at someone else, no matter how slimy it had made me feel, I'd played along.

I'd been a doormat. No wonder Bridget and Tiffany had been such bitches to me. I'd let them. After Ethan disappeared, I'd never once stood up for myself. Not even over little things.

"You left me there." I didn't mean to sound so angry.

He squeezed me. "You heard what Dad said to me."

I remembered. His snarled ultimatum had chilled me. Something inside me had broken the day he made his priorities clear. "My roof, my rules. Bentley or nothing." The next week had been a haze of moments I wanted so hard to forget.

"And I picked nothing." Then he'd walked out the door and never come back. "Because I had to. These might've been the worst two years of my life, but if I had to make that choice again, between Bentley and the Marines, I wouldn't change it. Sometimes, Cog, you have to choose yourself. It's not selfish when it's about survival."

Weeks later, a big envelope had come, addressed to Mom. Ethan had sent his Marines portrait to her. He hadn't put a note inside, just an eight by ten photograph of him smiling in uniform. Another few weeks after that, I'd gotten my first letter from him, and we began two years of writing to each other without saying anything.

"I'm tired."

"Me too," Ethan said. "But I promised you an explanation. The recruiter shot me down. He showed me the requirements for the flight training program, and my test scores didn't even come close. There was a chance I could overcome it, but according to those scores, he thought I'd do a lot better with a different focus. That's it."

"You gave up."

He sucked in a deep breath through his nose and let it out. With that air, he deflated enough to notice. "I gave up."

Ethan had never seemed so...human before. My big brother had always been bigger than life and twice as awesome. He learned to make macaroni and cheese when he was nine because I wanted it for dinner and our parents ran late that night. He taught me how to do my own laundry when I ran out of clothes and no one washed them for me. He showed me how math really worked with candies.

He gave up on his dream while still goading me to fulfill mine.

I wrapped my arms around his neck and hugged the man who'd been more of a father to me than our dad.

CHAPTER 13

"This will feel weird at first," Ethan said as he helped me climb into my pod.

My pod sat beside Mendez's. Blood coral had engulfed him, leaving an M-shaped vein symbol at the end. I worried about how to breathe inside.

I paused with one knee on the foam-like bed. Clutching his hand, I gulped. "Shouldn't I take off my boots first?"

"Not necessary."

"Are you sure?"

"Yes." He took my elbow and used it to nudge me off-balance.

To avoid falling, I slipped my other knee onto the bed. "Hey!" Jerk.

"You're stalling. If you're not really tired, we can go back to the Mess and stuff some food into you."

"It just doesn't seem…safe."

Ethan huffed. "We've been using these things for a while. If anything bad was going to happen, it would've happened by now."

That logic offered no room for argument. I sighed and wiggled into the pod. From the outside, it seemed too short to hold me, but my boots didn't reach the end.

Leaning over me, Ethan smiled. "Good night, Cog."

Like he'd done a million times before, he kissed my forehead. "I'll see you in the morning."

I wished I had a blanket he could tuck under my chin. "Good night."

"Akata, she's ready to sleep." Ethan squeezed my hand one last time, then let go.

The blood coral rose from the edges of the pod to engulf me. As it met over my head, I saw Ethan still smiling. At least nothing had gone wrong that he could tell? I still had to force myself not to squirm. Claustrophobia had never been a problem for me, but the coral pressed close, like when it had given me clothing. This time, though, it conformed to my head.

Without Ethan's assurances, I would've screamed. The coral touched my face, warm and suffocating, except that I could still breathe. Had I woken before like this without noticing? As the coral crowded my vision, I closed my eyes. When it touched my nose, the faint scent of hot cocoa surprised me. My ears filled with a quiet, soothing hum.

Warmth enveloped me from head to toe. Even if I'd wanted to stay awake, I couldn't have. The darkness behind my eyelids clouded with static. I felt weightless and supported at the same time, like drifting underwater without the feeling of drowning.

When the static cleared, I stood in Mr. Mackie's office again. He smiled at me like Ethan had. Would cyborg wolfmen torment me again? I braced myself for what I'd see before checking my body. Like the last time I'd been in this situation, my whole body had bloated like sausages. Lumps of fat squished beneath my clothes. Skin touched skin and made me squirm. This sucked.

"Hello, Miss Harper."

I scanned the room, not sure if I'd fallen asleep, transitioned to a different level of Hell, or hallucinated. Everything seemed in place, as I remembered it from school. Mr. Mackie didn't smell like strawberry cheesecake, but he hadn't before either, until his head blew up.

"Hi. How do I talk to Akata?"

His smile broadened. "What do you want from her?"

"I have questions. I want to understand how the facility works, among other things." Reaching out, I poked the desk. It felt solid, like real wood.

Mr. Mackie gestured to the door. "I think you will find her where you expect."

Because that made sense, I guess. "Okay." Using the door, I waved goodbye to Mr. Mackie. He probably represented something for me, though I had no idea what. Friendly authority, maybe.

I stepped into a school hallway, with locker banks, student art on the walls, and the usual signage mural on the floor with arrows pointing down each hallway. The normal words on the arrows, things like "cafeteria" and "gym," had all been replaced with "FACILITY."

Akata had a weird sense of humor, if she had one at all.

Not sure if it made a difference which direction I chose, I stood in the center of the arrows. Would the places the arrows normally pointed to affect anything? I didn't want to talk to Akata surrounded by pizza and donuts, so the cafeteria seemed wrong. The gym meant other girls staring at my freak body. In the math and science department, I'd been a huge disappointment. I'd never done well in anything.

The least unpleasant part of high school had been the one art class I'd taken during my sophomore year. Ms. Becker had been nice, at least. No one had expected anything more than stick figures and glued-together collages. I'd gotten one of my few As in that class.

At the other high school in our district, they offered robotics classes I would've killed to take. Mine, on the other hand, had a champion debate team and better-than-average football team. But I didn't need to be bussed across town for robotics because I was going to be an accountant or a lawyer.

I headed toward the art, drama, and English

departments. The hallway matched my memories, complete with the stuffed debate trophy case. Posters for a theater production shifted, rotating between all the plays I'd noticed the drama club offering over the years. Bridget had been the Drama Queen for our senior year. She'd picked and starred in all three plays, after picking and starring in two of three the previous year.

Rumors said she goaded the drama teacher into cheating on his wife with her. As her second best friend, I couldn't say if she had or not. Jokes full of innuendo had never been proven or confirmed, and her boyfriend didn't seem to care. Anything to get between Bridget's legs, or so Andy had once said.

I reached the room where I'd taken that art class and opened the door. Instead of a classroom, I found the open airlock in the outer wall of the facility. Dim red light glowed in a metal corridor. To my surprise, Madison stood inside with a polite, pleasant smile. Her outline glowed white like she had an aura.

Madison held out a hand to me. "I am happy to meet you, Cog."

For several beats, I stared at her. Ethan's nickname for me falling out of Madison's mouth made no sense.

Her expression clouded and contracted into a frown. "This shape is too confusing for you." She rippled. Madison's blonde curls faded, replaced by brown hair with a wide curl at the end. Her favorite blue dress shifted into a black catsuit.

Diana Rigg as Emma Peel raised her brow at me. "Is this better?"

After encountering so much that made no sense, I didn't know what to say. I did, though, have a guess about this. "Akata?"

She beamed at me. "Yes!"

"Uh, okay." I didn't mind having Diana Rigg as my escort, but I still didn't really understand. "Why don't you just show up like you look?"

Her smile dimmed. "Harper, Mendez, Nash, and Baldwin find my true appearance disturbing. You are human like them. I do not wish to disturb you."

"Oh." Freaks unite. "I don't think I'd mind, but however you want to look is fine. Hey, can I change how I look here?"

Akata's smile faded to a blank line. "You appear in your dreams as you see yourself."

How unfair. I crossed my thick, wobbly arms and tried not to let that bother me. I had things to do, after all. Important things.

"Fine. What can you explain to me about the facility?"

Akata offered her hand again. "I can show you everything the men have seen."

I took her strong, thin hand with my gross one and followed her into the ship. "The floor has an electrified grate embedded in it. Which I don't understand, because the whole thing is metal. Shouldn't I have been electrocuted by touching the floor with my finger, and not just the grate?"

"The Enemy mixes metal ores with coral to create a non-conductive material with enough strength to use as flooring. The outer shell of the facility is made of steel, but the interior is a coral-steel alloy."

Watching the walls instead of Akata, I crinkled my brow. "How do you know that?"

"My vessel did not spring forth immediately prior to encountering the human men. I have had other passengers."

"Cool. I'm guessing you've never met any of these Enemy people?"

"No, I have not. They are a mystery to me. But I am familiar with their handiwork. You humans are not the first species the enemy has brought to fight the Lepiku—the people your men refer to as cyborg wolfmen. I have taken members of two other races as passengers."

We reached a four-way intersection. One direction offered only complete darkness. The other two continued with dim red light. Akata stopped and gestured for me to choose.

"What's that way?" I pointed at the darkness.

"Your men have never gone that way. I have no information."

"Not even from those two prior species?"

Akata shook her head. "Your men are the first to return to the facility of their own free will. When return is involuntary, the visual information I can access is too disjointed to include."

I objected to her calling the guys mine, but didn't have a reason to complain. It made sense to Akata, which meant neither of us had to deal with trying to come up with a better option. Besides, I didn't want to be a problem.

"I want to see everything, so I guess let's go this way first."

CHAPTER 14

Hallway after hallway led to dark end after dark end. The guys had no idea about anything they saw, offering Akata little or no context for anything. Several areas lacked detail. Other parts had excessive detail, but nothing worth investigating further.

I saw a room where the guys had spent time as prisoners of the enemy people. According to Akata, they'd waited in that box for at least a day. She showed me how the dark, blank cube looked with twelve men stuck inside. They'd barely had room to sit, let alone lie down and rest.

At the end of the tour, we stood in the control room for the wormhole device. Lights, buttons, levers, and dials covered a wide control panel with a large screen. Glass or something similar made up a wall shielding the control panel without preventing access to it, like an observation shield. Through it, we could see a large, silvery mirror with a raised platform beside it. A wide ramp led to the floor. Mounted on the wall opposite the mirror, a bulky, gun-like object pointed at it.

"How did they activate the device?" We needed better words for this stuff than "facility" and "device," but I had no brilliant ideas.

"Baldwin did this." She stood in front of the control panel and did what looked a lot like mashing the keyboard.

He'd flipped switches, pushed buttons, and even thumped the whole panel with a fist. At no time did he touch the screen, which surprised me. "When he pushed this button, it made noise. He stopped touching things at that point, and it functioned."

He'd gotten lucky, it sounded like. To use the device properly, I'd need to spend some time checking under its hood. Figuring it all out might take a long time. But the device could have been programmed with a reverse mode. In that case, I wouldn't have to rewire anything.

When I got there, I wanted to attack the screen as my first priority. Maybe it wouldn't make sense, but screens usually meant visuals, and I could work with visuals.

"Was Ethan in that room?" I pointed to the mirror.

"Yes, Harper stood in front of the mirror. They hoped to send a message."

"Sure." I furrowed my brow. "How? I mean, they didn't have any idea how it worked. What made them think they could get a message out?"

"I will show you." Akata wiped her hand over the glass. In her wake, the wall changed into a dirty mirror mounted on a dirt-colored wall.

The surface reflected twelve soldiers, including Ethan, Mendez, Nash, and Baldwin. Several checked their weapons and swapped clips of bullets. One wrapped a bandage around another's arm. Ethan watched the outside through a ragged curtain over a window.

Nash used the mirror to squish a piece of glass out of a cut on his cheek. The mirror's surface rippled with static, just like mine had. Instead of resolving into Ethan's face, it pulsed with crackling, multicolored light.

Like I had, Nash touched the mirror. Somehow, he whisked the entire group with him. The device probably swept up all living creatures within a radius of the target mirror. Maybe they'd brought rats or tarantulas still scuttling in the room.

Ew.

Akata slashed her hand through the image, replacing it with the glass wall. "Everything after that is confused and jumbled. The mechanical creatures used electrical discharges to make your men behave in certain ways."

I realized Akata had put all of this together by compositing their memories. The idea of wandering through the guys' memories bothered me. Thoughts were supposed to stay private. Akata didn't seem to have any concept of privacy. With no other way to get the information, though, I plowed onward.

To myself, I pledged not to ask for personal memories. The composites would suffice.

"What do the mechanical creatures look like?"

A six-foot robot trundled through the open doorway on tank-like treads. Four long, folding arms, each mounted on one side of a cube, ended with two pairs of pincers. Below the cube, a dark, glassy sphere rotated. It anchored to the treads by a stubby column.

"The pincers can either grab or emit a shock," Akata said.

Stalking around the robot, I wished I could take one apart. The use of treads interested me because humans had recently figured out how to have a stable robot on two legs. These aliens had mastered wormhole technology. Two-legged robots sounded easier. I remembered something Ethan had said about gravity and thought suction cups or bumpers would've worked even better.

"How does the facility generate power? Or the mechanical creatures?" How had Akata never picked up on the guys calling them robots?

"The outer shell of the facility is wired to disperse light energy from the nearby star and collect the resulting free electrons. How the mechanical creatures receive and use the generated power is unclear."

I recognized the technical definition of solar power

and nodded. "Maybe that's what the wire grate in the floor is for."

"This is possible. No one has examined the mechanical creatures with care. They may have additional, as yet unknown features."

As I listened to Akata speak more and more, she made me think of an android. Ethan had referred to her as a brain and said she'd caught a cold. That meant she had organic parts. I wanted to see her true shape and know more about her. Later, though. For now, I had a mission.

I pushed the button on the control panel, but had no idea why. It did nothing, of course. "Can you show me what the device does?"

Akata nodded. The base of the gun-like object spun with a whirring noise. Its thick barrel pulled back like a gun recoiling from firing, then a crackling bolt of white light shot toward the mirror. When the bolt hit, the silvery surface rippled and glowed with a tiny sun. The barrel convulsed again, firing another bolt, this time yellow. The glow enlarged and took on a yellow tint. After that, it fired a third bolt of blue, a fourth of reddish purple, and a fifth of black.

With each bolt, the glow grew and its color shifted, becoming a mixture. When the black bolt fired, I expected it to overwhelm the rest and turn the whole thing to black. Instead, it wiped the color away. The glow returned to white and grew to about three feet in width.

The image disappeared with a wave of Akata's hand.

"Wait, why did you stop it?"

"I have learned that humans find seeing themselves in this fashion upsetting."

I blinked. "Oh." She only had the guys' memories, so of course this one included me coming through the wormhole. Suddenly, I wondered if my robe had come open. Had they all taken a good look before Ethan picked me up? Did I want to know?

No, I didn't.

"Okay, that's fair." I tried to think about something else and realized what hadn't been part of our tour earlier. "I didn't see the parts where the guys ripped pieces out of the facility. Where did that happen?"

"I do not yet know. They have not yet slept enough since it happened."

"I thought Ethan was going to sleep right after me. How long does it take you to get stuff from their memories?"

"Whatever they learned today, I will be able to share with you during your next sleep cycle."

"Oh. Hm. Okay." I tried to bite back my disappointment. Akata could only do things as fast as she could do them, and me whining wouldn't change that. She had five brains to interact with, after all.

I shifted gears, trying to come up with other questions she could answer now. The more I knew, the more I could come up with ideas while awake.

"Do you know what the gray material is?" I lifted my hand and tried to show her the box with the fans inside. Instead of a solid image, I produced a wispy, translucent version.

Akata cocked her head to one side. "I cannot process this image fast enough for you now. Explain it to me."

For now, I gave up trying to make an image. Tomorrow night, I'd try again. "They pried off a metal-coral plate and ripped out pieces of the facility's innards. The gray stuff held the coral-metal plates together. It's rubbery and hard to cut."

"Ah. It is coral without an alloy. The gray variety, or common coral, grows in many places, but it cannot withstand space like the blood variety."

"Is it really space coral? I mean, is that what non-humans call it?"

"There is no appropriate human word or concept for this creature known to your men. Mendez supplied the term and your men accepted it. Based upon their understanding of coral, it is reasonably close to accurate."

That explanation made sense to me. "Does your coral have to be connected to you to do anything? Like, could I take a handful off the ship and expect it to be able to function? Could it use me as its brain instead of you?"

Akata tipped her head to the side and linked at me. "I do not know. None of your men could handle the complex processes required to direct the coral. You might be able to. Your mind is different from theirs in subtle ways. They are driven more by instinct and reflex, where you seem to have a greater focus on intellect."

Thank you, Akata, for reminding me that I had an alien rooting through my head.

"The smallest amount of coral that can survive separated from the main colony is this much." She held up her hands to suggest a size similar to a shoebox. "If you are able to interface with the coral, I suggest practicing before attempting to accomplish anything of import. Should your brain prove complementary enough, I will be able to direct the coral myself and communicate with you through it."

I had my plans for the next few days, so it seemed.

CHAPTER 15

"Absolutely not," Ethan said the next morning. He gave me a look like I'd asked to dance naked on the table.

We sat around the table in the Mess, eating food resembling Belgian waffles with a sweet, chunky orange sauce on top. The waffles, though, didn't taste like waffles, and the sauce had nothing to do with oranges. I thought it tasted like multigrain toast with mixed berry jam.

The fat fell into my gut like lead and I couldn't do anything about it. Except exercise. I could exercise a ton later. We had nothing else to do anyway.

I frowned at Ethan. "Why not?"

"It's too dangerous."

My protector let my personal safety blind him to the bigger picture. No one else did that for me. I smiled because I couldn't stop myself.

"I need to see things for myself. Akata tried to show me the interior of the facility, but you guys don't know anything about engineering. There's no way to tell what a lot of that stuff is for. You all just see hallways with nothing special about them."

"C'mon, Harper," Nash said. "What're you gonna do? Stick her in a box? She's stuck here with us. She oughta pull her weight."

"This isn't a debate," Ethan snapped. He glared at Nash

first, then me.

I wilted. He'd never yelled or snapped at me before. Whenever he got angry, he'd always stalk out of the room rather than show it.

"It should be," Mendez said. "She has ideas. What if one of them works?"

Ethan scowled like no one had ever disagreed with him before. "She can give us instructions and we can do whatever she needs on the facility."

Mendez rolled his eyes. "Don't be an ass. You know as well as I do that when a mission goes fubar, you want the expert right there to deal with it."

"Didn't I say this wasn't a debate?" Ethan flicked his gaze to Baldwin and Nash.

Baldwin shrugged.

Nash held up his hands in surrender. "I just wanna go home."

"Me too," Mendez said. "I say let her do whatever she wants, however she wants. New person, new ideas, new things to try."

Baldwin patted Ethan on the shoulder. "They got a point."

Ethan grumbled something that sounded like "mutiny" as he shoved a bite of waffle into his mouth.

"I don't want to go to the facility right now," I said, hoping to defuse him. My idea for using the blood coral seemed sure to annoy him, so I decided not to talk about it. "I need more time with Akata first. Two or three nights."

"Maybe we can trade with the greenies for a smaller gun for her," Mendez said. "You know how to shoot?"

Ethan shot me a look I didn't understand. He didn't glare, but I thought he offered some warning. What he wanted to warn me about, I had no idea.

"No. Mom and Dad don't like guns."

"Eh." Mendez shrugged. "It's not hard. Hold the grip, aim the open end at the target, squeeze the trigger, expect recoil. I can show you how to aim."

"How're you gonna get the greenies to understand you want a weapon?" Nash asked.

"Show 'em one," Baldwin said. He stuffed his last bite into his mouth and stood with his plate and fork.

Mendez nodded. "Yeah, that'll work. C'mon, Harper. We'll go see the greenies, get her a weapon, and hide out while she comes up with a plan. And when we get to the facility, I'll stay on her six the whole time while you guys try to distract the robots."

"I still don't like this idea." At least Ethan sounded resigned.

"Sucks to be you," Mendez said with a cheesy smile.

"Shut up," Ethan groused.

As I sat there, listening to the guys talk, I realized I didn't understand my brother anymore. He still did and said things I expected, but he'd changed a lot. I wondered how they'd all adjust when they got home. Maybe they'd all be miserable without the freedom of a spaceship at their disposal, or maybe they'd all be happy to have a chain of command to work with again.

Then I wondered how *I'd* handle it. Akata answered my questions without judging me. Few of my teachers had ever done that. Most had seemed to slog through their day, droning about their subject like they wanted to chuck it all and head for the beach.

On second thought, that might've been me.

I tried to remember the last time I'd asked a question in class and came up blank. Instead, I remembered doodling in my notebook, writing notes for my latest project, checking my phone under my desk, or pretending to read a textbook while actually reading an engineering trade magazine from the library. Teachers had asked me questions. I'd flubbed the answers and looked like an idiot.

My mediocre grades weren't a mystery. I could've tried, but I never did.

"You going to sit here for a while?" Mendez asked.

I blinked. Ethan and Nash had somehow left the room without me noticing. Mendez had dropped off his plate and fork already, and he sat beside me. My plate still sat on the table. I also hadn't noticed myself eating the whole thing. Worse, I could see the lines where I'd swiped my finger through the orange topping to lick it up.

Groaning, I pushed my plate away. This fat pig needed to purge, but I didn't know where to do it. Come to think of it, I needed a toilet all around. Why hadn't I needed one an hour ago, when I first woke up?

"What's the matter, chica?" Mendez tugged the fork out of my hand and set it on the plate.

"Nothing." I shook my head and thought about what I could do besides talk to Mendez.

Mendez nodded. "Are you sure?"

He seemed sincere, which made me wary. No one cared that much except Ethan. Even if Mendez did want to know, though, I didn't want to talk about it.

"Where's the bathroom? Ethan showed me the shower, but that's not what I could use right now." I braced for him to keep prying.

"Same place. Ask and Akata gives."

He stood, giving me space, and picked up my plate. I didn't know what to think. Most guys, given a brush-off, leaned in. Andy always got handsy when I told him no. Then again, he got handsy no matter what. Leaving Madison alone with him had been mean to her. I was a terrible person.

"Thanks." I scooted off my chair and rushed to the shower.

Within minutes, water flowed over my naked body. Akata made me a hole to use. Sitting on my knees, I stared into a dark pit. Everything about this felt wrong. I needed the porcelain bowl. I also needed to purge. Once, at a party, the bathrooms had all been in use when I'd stumbled around the house, panicking. My only option had been a line of shrubs in the front yard. Like now, I'd stared at the darkness in horror, thinking about the fat congealing in my thighs and gut. Then I'd fled the party rather than deal with it.

I needed the porcelain bowl. Akata didn't have one. The longer I stayed here, the fatter I'd get. Everything I ate would cling. Dark, oily goo swam through my body, pouncing on any available spot and multiplying. My body felt bloated and gross. At least water sluiced away my filth.

Once I'd used the hole the way Akata meant, I scrubbed myself as close to raw as I could with nothing more than my hands. Akata needed loofahs or scrubby puffs. She also needed soap. Despite that, when I asked her to turn off the water and clothe me again, I felt as clean as anyone who'd gorged herself like a pig could.

Faced with the choices of sleep, exercise, or sitting in the Mess, I leaned against the wall and covered my face. This ship and its remove from Earth had seemed like Heaven at first. In less than a day, it already pressed close, crowding me. Ethan had pulled me through to a prison.

I heard the guys' voices as a buzzing murmur coming from the weight room. They laughed. How could they find anything funny here? This ship didn't have enough space. Unless it did, and I only had to ask? Hadn't Ethan said something about having my own room if I wanted one when he showed me the sleeping pods?

"Akata, can I have a private room?"

On the wall beside me, white veins pulsed into an arrow. It pointed at a blank wall to the side. As I watched, a seam opened. Like Mendez had said, ask and Akata gives.

I stepped inside and patted the wall next to the seam. Akata closed it. Privacy accomplished, I didn't know what to do with it. One thing came to mind after a minute or two of blank silence.

"Akata, I want to try interfacing with a smaller piece of you."

The blood coral writhed. I touched the wall, and the

surface wriggled under my hand. It climbed over my fingers and kept going, enveloping my right arm. It felt a lot like like putting on a wet swimsuit.

That idea made my stomach clench. I didn't have a swimsuit-ready body. Especially not after eating two full meals here.

The coral separated from the wall and forced me back a step. Standing in the center of the small room with my arm covered in living blood coral, I tried not to panic.

No one else could see me, so it didn't matter how I looked. I could be as fat, ugly, and freakish as ever, and no one would care.

Except me.

Faint buzzing tickled the edge of my hearing. The coral climbed up my shoulder to touch my neck. Sparks jolted my spine. Delicate fingers prodded my brain. The buzzing grew louder until I thought I might go crazy.

Then it all stopped.

"Can you hear me, Emma?"

I blinked like a moron again and turned around, looking for the speaker. "Yes?"

"It is Akata. Interface is complete and successful. Your mind is well suited to this. The calibration went swiftly and succeeded more than I expected."

An alien hive mind liked my brain. "Uh. Great? I guess?"

"I require access to the base of your neck, but you do not need to sleep to interact with me."

"Oh. Cool." What could I do with remote access to Akata? Record everything so she could create holographic images for me to analyze. Maybe other things. "Can you translate for me while I'm talking to someone?"

"Only if I have data on the language."

"What happens if this coral on my arm is hit by something?"

"The outer shell is capable of withstanding space even

without the forcefield I generate. There is little that can damage or remove it without my consent."

I had access to body armor. No, I had access to kickass, intelligent body armor. "Can you do this for the guys even if they can't interface with you?"

"Without a successful interface, I cannot move the coral with your body. An unlinked coral covering would restrict movement too much to provide any value."

With indestructible body armor, Ethan lost his reason not to let me join them on a trip into the facility. I could poke things. Try things. Do stuff.

Get us home.

Instead of running to Ethan, I took my time experimenting. Akata made me a full body covering. She had to leave my face exposed so I could see. If I could find her a screen and camera option, she could create a faceplate, but I didn't see that happening.

"In the event you are exposed to open space, I can cause the coral to cover your face, which will afford you about five minutes before you suffer the effects of asphyxiation."

Note to self—don't step into open space without a way to get back.

Good advice for anyone, really.

CHAPTER 16

Ethan frowned at me in the kitchen. The guys sat around the table, playing cards again. They'd all set down their hands when I came into the room covered in blood coral armor. At my request, Akata had smoothed the outer surface without conforming to my shape too much.

I felt like Mrs. Peel.

I also felt like Ethan remembered me as a little girl who needed help and rescue, and couldn't quite wrap his head around an Emma who could do things besides match outfits.

"I dare you to argue anymore," Mendez said. He grinned like he didn't want Ethan to see it but couldn't help himself.

"I'm not saying I want to go fight robots or cyborg wolfmen, or anything else." At my mental request, Akata withdrew the coral from my hand. I held it out so Ethan could take it. "I'm just saying I'm not helpless. Give me a small gun just in case, and I promise I won't go off on my own."

"A ship approaches," Akata said. "It is consistent with those employed by the lepiku. I would expect an imminent attack."

Had to open my big mouth. "Akata says—"

The ship wobbled to the side. I only stayed on my feet because the coral armor anchored me to the floor. Everyone else fell off their chairs or hit the table.

"Weapons," Ethan barked.

The armor closed around my hand again. I followed the guys as they scrambled to their feet and ran for the guns.

"Cyborg wolfmen attacking," I said. As if they couldn't figure that out on their own.

"This ship does not have any weapons," Akata told me. She must have seen the idea in my head. Nothing creepy about that.

"So how does this work?"

"Boarding," Mendez said. "They're going to try to board the ship."

"Their weapons are not capable of causing serious damage to the ship, but the energy involved forces me to cycle the power long enough for them to catch us and force open the airlock. The airlock is a weak point because I have to maintain the gap even when it is shut. This is a complicated matter, one we can discuss later if you wish to know details."

"Thanks, Akata." I didn't need to know the details. Knowing the basics helped more than enough. "How can I help?"

"Stay out of sight!" Ethan reached the gun room and passed out rifles.

I didn't know what I'd expected him to say. Too weak to lift a weapon and unfamiliar with combat, I had nothing to offer. If I never even watched, though, I'd never learn anything.

The guys lined up, rifles ready, watching the airlock. I stood at the nearest corner and peeked around it. Akata anchored me in place.

We waited.

Bright light punched through the airlock, forcing the seal open. Ethan and the boys opened fire without a word between them. Green bolts flew through the air, in one direction only, and filled the hallway with video game laser noises.

At the airlock, I saw a boot step onto the floor. The

bolts flared in front of the owner, pulsing too bright to see the rest of the invader. I didn't need to see the rest, though. I recognized the shape of the boot.

Andy as a lepiku had worn that boot. He'd come for me.

An androgynous voice spoke in a strange language full of guttural barks and long vowels. Some of it sounded like a question, the rest like shouting and threats.

Though I didn't want to know what he said, I took a deep breath and asked, "Akata, did you understand that? Can you tell me what he said?"

"No, I do not know that language."

Thank goodness.

"Emma, get out of there!" Ethan charged forward.

The other three guys followed him. I slid down the wall and let Akata anchor me in place where I couldn't see anything.

Whatever happened, it sounded horrible. People grunted. Bones crunched. Someone screamed. Mendez shouted. Rifles fired.

I covered my ears and slid down the wall to the floor. With all my heart, I wanted the fighting to stop.

Nash's hand gripped the corner beside me. He dragged himself into view. "Emma, help me." His voice rasped with pain.

Doing everything I could to not look, I took Nash's hand, braced against the wall, and pulled him toward me.

"Take him to a sleep pod," Akata said as she used the suit to help me stand. "I can repair him."

"I can't lift him!"

Though I pulled as hard as I could, Nash still did most of the work. He pushed off the wall. As he maneuvered himself around the corner, I realized his leg dragged at an odd angle. A broken leg. He needed a…a…splint?

"Emma, please calm down." Akata sounded so cool and confident. Like the guys. Like everyone except me.

"Akata! Get us out of here!" Ethan bellowed.

The ship lurched sideways. I fell on my side. For once, falling didn't hurt. Thank you, blood coral bodysuit.

Mendez and Baldwin rushed around the corner. Baldwin picked up Nash by his armpits while Mendez scooped me off the floor.

"Are you okay?" Mendez asked. His earthy scent blocked out the metallic tinge of Akata's air.

I blinked at him, then I turned my head to watch Baldwin hustle to the sleep pods with Nash. "Fine," I said.

Ethan muttered words I couldn't hear as he approached. He turned the corner with two rifles in his arms and saw us. "Put my sister down," he snapped.

"Settle down, Sarge." Mendez set me on my feet and helped me balance. "She fell and was in the way."

"That doesn't mean you have to pick her up."

Mendez raised his hands. "I'm not copping a feel, Harper."

"I'm fine," I said. "You can stop trying to protect me from the dangerous bad boys on your team anytime."

Ethan glared at me. I didn't know why. He made me want to cry and scream at the same time.

"Do you think I'm still a virgin? And it's your job to keep me that way?"

He flinched like I slapped him. "What?"

"I'm eighteen, Ethan. An adult. I can make decisions for myself. You don't get to police my body." My gross, icky body that only a gross, icky guy like Andy ever wanted.

We glared at each other more. I got the feeling he wanted to say something, but he stayed quiet.

"Whatever," he grumbled. He turned his back on me and stomped down the hallway.

Mendez and I stood in the hallway for a long few minutes, not saying anything. I rubbed my arm, not sure why I felt cold under the coral suit. He rocked on his heels and swung his arms so his hands touched, over and over.

Baldwin stepped out of the sleep pod room, looked us over, and walked in the other direction.

"I really didn't mean anything by picking you up."

"It's cool."

"But you are a good-looking woman."

I blushed and tried not to squirm. "Am not. I'm gross."

"Nah, just a little too skinny, chica. C'mon. Let's put some food into you. Excitement always makes me hungry."

Like magic, he said food and my belly growled. "I'm not—"

"Hungry, I know." Mendez huffed and grinned. "I'm starting to think that means you don't like any of us."

I froze. My pulse sped. "I'm tired," I stammered, falling on my usual excuse when I didn't want to deal with a guy. "I'm going to go do the sleep pod thing."

Mendez touched my shoulder as I turned. I flinched. He snatched back his hand like I'd burned it.

"Hey, I didn't mean anything by that." I recognized the voice of a guy worried he'd lost his chance to get into my pants. "I just want to make sure you get enough to eat. It's important. Interfacing with Akata uses energy. You'll waste away to nothing if you're not careful. Especially now that you're doing it through this suit thing."

Had I stumbled into the best weight-loss method ever? Maybe! "I'll have something when I get up."

"You're hungry now, chica. I'll make you a noodle bowl. Sleep on a happy belly, not an empty one."

"Worst advice ever," I grumbled. I whirled and stalked to the pod room. Everyone knew sleeping made your stomach work slower. The longer it took, the more of the bad stuff your cells absorbed. Sleeping on a full stomach made anybody fatter. Even if you only ate kale and bean sprouts.

I grimaced. Who knew what the food here actually had in it? They traded for things they didn't understand from people they couldn't communicate with, and expected good nutrition. By magic or something, probably.

More likely, though, they didn't care. So long as they built muscles and kept going like machines, what different did it make? Ugh. Thinking about how much Ethan ate made me sick. In my head, I watched him shovel a ton of food into his mouth, and the memory made me want my porcelain bowl.

I hugged myself, unable to feel my flesh through the coral. "Akata, can you remove the armor?"

Though she said nothing, the coral wriggled down my body to rejoin the floor. In its absence, I rubbed the flab on my upper arms. I felt like me, and me felt disgusting. Maybe I wanted the coral suit after all.

As I climbed into a sleep pod, I noticed Mendez watching me from the doorway. He flashed me a weak smile and a small wave. I didn't return either.

The pod closed over me. Thank goodness, because I didn't know what else to do.

CHAPTER 17

For the next several hours, Akata helped me practice using the coral armor in my sleep. We ran through exercises to train my neurons and create muscle memory, or so she said. I didn't see how we could do that in my sleep, but I had no reason not to trust her.

When I woke, Nash also sat up. He put his feet on the floor while I watched. No one had splinted or wrapped his leg. I also noticed Akata had changed my outfit from black to light pink. In my sleep. Nope, nothing creepy going on.

Nash grinned at me. "I'm fine. Good as new."

"Your leg was broken."

"Yeah. Akata fixed it." He stood. "She's amazing. I gotta admit, when we go home, I'm gonna miss her. Not gonna miss any of the rest of this, but her? Yeah. One day, when I'm sitting on the porch of my Momma's house, sipping lemonade in heat thick as honey, I'm gonna think back to healing a broken leg overnight and kinda miss that."

Nash ran in place for a few steps, raising his knees high. He didn't wince or favor the leg at all.

"That's amazing." I wondered if Akata had found some kind of disorder or something in me that caused the static, since I hadn't seen it as much in the past couple of days. Maybe she had a way to fix things like that too, just in slow motion. Something like a broken bone seemed simpler than a deeper problem.

"You up for food?"

On cue, my stomach growled. Stupid thing. I hated it more than ever.

"Sounds like yes." He grinned and held out a hand to me. "You ain't tried the oatmeal yet, have you?"

Oatmeal didn't sound bad. I took his hand and let him lead me to the Mess. "Is it made with skim milk?"

Nash laughed. "Listen to you, silly woman. Like they got cows here. The best part, though, is these little red bits bobbing in the stuff. I don't know what in heckfire they are, but I do know they taste like manna straight from God's hand to my mouth."

I wrinkled my nose as we entered the Mess. I heard the other guys chatting in the weight room. "That sounds bad for you."

"Naw." He took me to a chair and held my hand while I sat, then let go. "Akata, two bowls of oatmeal, please. Akata makes sure we only get stuff we need. She gave us samples the first few times, see? We showed it to the greenies, and they traded us coral sticks for more of the same. No worries. It all comes in boxes."

"Boxes." I hadn't eaten anything out of a box in years. Not since Ethan left. "You mean none of this is fresh?"

"You think we grow it on the ship or something?" He laughed. "There's no free-range, organic, cage-free, non-GMO anything out here. We eat because if we don't, we starve. Nobody starves on Harper's watch."

Every new thing I learned about the food made it worse. "That doesn't seem very healthy."

"You're kinda overly concerned about that." He carried two steaming bowls to the table and set one in front of me with a spoon.

I didn't like the direction of this conversation. Picking up the spoon, I prodded a red piece the size of my fingernail swimming in a sea of tan and beige sludge. If the bowl didn't have milk, it probably didn't have oats either. The oatmeal smelled like sugar and spice and everything nice. I prayed for the red things not to taste like strawberries.

"Go on." Nash waved his spoon at my bowl, then dunked it into his own. "It's good stuff. Akata takes good care of us."

Watching him stuff a bite of food into his mouth make me salivate. Because I'm a gross cow. That thought made me wonder if I could be milked, which led to all kinds of unpleasant places. I squirmed in my chair and set down my spoon.

Nash swallowed his mouthful and dunked his spoon into his bowl again. "You do know that you gotta eat, right? I mean, you seem confused on that point."

"I know." I set my hands in my lap. "I just don't want to eat this."

"It's made, so somebody better eat it. Wasting food is the worst sin we got out here." He sounded and looked so nonchalant while judging me.

I picked up the spoon again and dipped it into the oatmeal. With it half full, I touched it with my tongue to check the temperature. The tiny taste reminded me of thick ice cream, the slow-churned stuff they claimed had fewer calories than regular but tasted like it had a zillion more.

The whole spoonful made me whimper. I was wrong. It tasted better than that ice cream and cheesecake combined. Scooping more into my mouth, I discovered the red pieces dissolved and had a strawberry-like sweetness with a different fruity flavor and no seeds.

Before I knew it, my spoon scraped the empty bowl. The whole thing had gone down my gullet. I dropped the spoon into the bowl and pushed it away like that would somehow absolve me of all the calories.

"Told ya it was good." Nash grinned and sounded smug. He took both bowls to the hole and dropped them in. "Nothing better than a full belly to get you going."

I gripped the edges of the table, not sure what to do. Akata had no porcelain bowl. Whatever I'd eaten, I knew it had to be bad. Nothing good tasted like that. With every passing second, I felt my gut and thighs expanding. If I didn't purge soon, I'd swell like a balloon.

Where could I go? I didn't know. I'd already tried to purge in the shower. It didn't feel right. Maybe I could do it in that other kind of private room, except it didn't have the right thing either.

Akata, for all her benefits, trapped me in the worst kind of prison.

"Are you okay?" Nash set a hand on my shoulder.

I shrugged away from him and fled the room. Outside the door, I ran into Baldwin. He caught me and grunted. Like Andy. Like Tom.

Like every other guy, ever.

This time, I wriggled and fought. Like I should have every other time.

He squeaked a curse and let go. I shoved him aside and ran down the hall to the room with the chairs and screen. Why did I go to that room? It was there? I guess?

I hit the corner and curled up, sitting and hugging my knees. In the distance, I heard the guys talking. Their voices murmured, soft and low. They sounded normal, like people who didn't have any problems. All their confidence and competence made me feel even smaller and more pathetic.

They didn't need me for anything. Akata could do everything they really needed. Of all the people they could've accidentally brought through to this hellhole, it should've been a physicist or a linguist. An engineer. Someone with genuine skills who could help them.

Instead, they got me. A bloated, fat freak who couldn't even scrape a three for my GPA.

My body shook as I cried. The rest of the world— The rest of the universe could go away.

For a while, no one bothered me, not even Akata. Snot

smeared my clothes. I probably sounded hysterical. The guys wouldn't want to deal with that.

"Hey, Cog."

I lifted my head and saw Ethan sitting next to me. Everything about me must've looked terrible, because he didn't put an arm around my shoulders.

"I'm sorry," he said. "I should've thought more about how hard this would be on you. You needed more time to adjust, and I should've given it to you." He handed me a square of black cloth.

For a moment, I stared at the cloth, not sure why he offered it. It seemed such a weird thing to do. Then I realized he meant it as a handkerchief. I took it and wiped my face.

"I'm also sorry that I hurt you by leaving. I did it for me, because I didn't see any other options. Dad was pretty clear that I didn't have a place to stay if I didn't go to Bentley and do what he wanted. He wouldn't pay for any other school, and I knew I'd hate it there. I spent a good, solid month looking at work options. Trying to find something I could do with a high school diploma and make enough to take care of myself… That future didn't look too bright."

I blew my nose. "I already know all that. We talked about it before you left."

"Yeah. I guess maybe I thought you needed to hear it again." He draped an around around my shoulders.

Leaning into him, I wanted to stay like this forever. "Thanks."

"How do you feel about taking another run on the facility? We can wait if you want. I don't mean to pressure you into doing things before you're ready. If you need a few days, then we'll wait a few days. We can go meet with the greenies and get you a weapon, or just sit and talk, or whatever you want."

The sooner I sucked it up and got to work, the sooner we could go home. Besides, I didn't want to let Ethan down. He deserved an engineer or scientist, but he had me. The least

I could do was give him my best effort.

"I can do it. Let's meet with the greenies."

He smiled and squeezed my shoulders. "You're sure?"

"Yes, I'm sure."

CHAPTER 18

The viewscreen showed us nearing a wide asteroid field with stars in the background. To the left, another ship appeared on the screen. It looked like a stack of white clouds squished in a vise, with the vise still attached like a giant rudder.

Akata had sent a signal to call the greenies for trade. According to her, they transmitted a location and Akata took us there. Since we needed a restock soon anyway, Ethan had decided we'd get food while also getting a weapon for me. Something about two birds and one stone. Even if we had a plan to return to Earth, we prepared for that plan to fail or take longer than expected.

As we neared the ship, I wondered what Akata looked like from the outside. The other ship seemed enormous. Not that I had a frame of reference. No part of Akata showed on the screen, and the visual didn't include a handy scale ruler.

"Take off the Akata suit," Ethan said. He flicked two fingers, indicating everyone should follow him out of the room.

"Why?" I trooped down the hallway beside him with the rest of the guys behind us. "She might be able to translate for us in real time."

"Because we don't want them to think we're going to try attacking. And we're better off if no one knows you can wear the coral." He patted my shoulder. "Think of it like a secret weapon."

"I am not certain I agree with his rationale," Akata said into my brain, "but I will defer to his judgment. The team can communicate well enough with this species already."

I remembered what Akata had said about the amount needed for an interface. "What if I'm only wearing part of it so I can still hear Akata? It could be small enough they wouldn't know what they're seeing."

In response, most of the coral suit slipped off my body. Akata left behind a narrow band around my neck and down my spine. The band flattened until it appeared smooth. Someone might mistake it for decoration.

Ethan looked me over and nodded. "That'll work."

Thank goodness, because I suspected Akata could still protect me so long as we stayed on the ship.

"What you are thinking, about me shrouding you with coral on a moment's notice, is correct. I am pleased this works."

Not half as pleased as me, I thought. Meeting aliens without some kind of protection sounded bad. Especially when the guys considered them less than friendly.

We trooped to the airlock. Baldwin, Nash, and Mendez each carried a laser rifle. Ethan held a small sack full of coral sticks. I stayed behind Mendez. Ethan had assigned him to guard me.

"The greenies are knocking. I am opening the airlock."

I didn't need to relay the message. The white veins changed beside the seam, then it opened.

Soft yellow light spilled from an entry made of white, metallic material. Two large creatures with striated green flesh stood in the entry for the other ship. I got my first good look at aliens.

Each being had two thick arms with curious seams along one side, like they could conceal objects inside their bodies. The pair of limbs bulged with rounded sections and tapered to multiple curled tendrils instead of hands or fingers. As far as I could tell, the creatures had no eyes, ears, or noses. In the center of what I'd call a torso, each had a bird-like beak. Five more limbs, each smooth and narrow, held them up like legs.

They looked like giant, animate versions of the pea plants Mom grew in our backyard. I wondered if they reproduced by flowering. Then I wondered if the babies came out of those weird seams on their arms as peas.

Beside the beaks, black straps secured a sleek silver box to each of their bodies. Loose white cloth hung from a waist-like indentation below their beaks and covered half their legs.

One greenie moved its beak and spoke with a low-pitched, reedy voice. To my surprise, an electronic voice said in English, "Welcome. We trade usual?"

"I am able to translate some of their language and can supply you with some words," Akata said. "Think what you wish to say and I will provide the closest match in phonemes for them."

"Food, yes," Ethan said. Instead of trying to say more, he made a plus sign with two fingers, then held up one finger. Reaching back, he tapped on Mendez's rifle, then moved his hands together to indicate something small.

Popping my head from behind Mendez, I held up my finger. Akata fed me syllables. I hoped I didn't mangle them too much.

"Small weapon for small being," I thought I said. "You can sell?"

Everyone stared at me. My cheeks burned. I wanted to curl up and die.

The greenie spoke. Whatever translated for him caught a few words, none of it helpful. Akata fed what she could into my brain. "You know some of our words now. This is good. Yes, we can sell you a weapon. How small is the being?"

"Me," I said, tapping my chest and stepping into view. "Strength small."

The greenie patted a tendril against his partner. Another tendril touched the box strapped to him. He spoke. We heard no translated words.

Those boxes were the translators. I wanted one.

"He is telling the other being to collect specific items and bring them. I believe the items are weapon types, but that is only a guess."

The second greenie used its leg tendrils to undulate deeper into the ship.

"How much did you bring to pay?" The translator picked up the final word.

Ethan stepped forward and opened the sack to show him.

The greenie stuck a tendril into the bag and rooted around. Thinking that made me notice his legs seemed like roots more than anything else.

"This is good." He removed his tendril from the bag. "Food and weapon for this."

Two other greenies joined us. One carried boxes. The other held four devices the size of pistols dangling from his various tendrils.

Nash and Baldwin took the boxes. Mendez nudged me forward. I gulped. Nearing the aliens, I noticed a light, sweet scent around them.

"Choose one," the primary greenie said.

Reaching for one of the devices topped my new list of weirdest thing I'd ever done. I felt even weirder touching a tendril without knowing how to refer to these people, though. "Name. Emma."

The primary greenie shivered. Not certain what that meant, I hoped for a positive sort of thing. Maybe he appreciated pleasantries. "Ohlioos."

"Good meeting, Ohlioos." The first device didn't fit my hand.

"Yes. Agreed, Emma."

I tried the second and didn't see how to make it work. Ohlioos would probably show me, and I expected Akata could figure it out, but I didn't want to have to learn something complex to defend myself. The third reminded me of a pistol, and it suited my hand. Using it seemed straightforward. Like Mendez had said, hold the grip, aim the open end at the target, squeeze the trigger, expect recoil.

Pointing to the gun-like weapon, I nodded. "This for Emma."

"Good choice." Akata paused in her translation. "I believe he is indicating it charges like the rifles. With some time to inspect it, I can discern all its facets."

Ohlioos took the sack from Ethan.

"Good trade," Ethan said. He bowed to Ohlioos.

"Good trade," Ohlioos agreed. To me he said, "I prefer trading with you, Emma. Come next time."

I blushed again and pointed to the translator on his body. "How can I have one?"

He paused and touched the box. When I nodded, Ohlioos said, "I carry no spares today. I will bring one for trade next time."

"Thank you." Following Ethan's example, I bowed to him. "Next time."

Ohlioos withdrew to his ship. Akata sealed the airlock. I had a gun.

"Good job, Cog." Ethan touched my shoulder.

The gun felt good in my hand for a moment. Then I remembered what guns did. I'd never seen anyone shot in real life, but it looked terrible on TV and in movies. Ethan expected me to use one to do that to someone. Holding the gun to the wall, I asked without words for Akata to take it.

Coral rippled out and engulfed it. The gun disappeared.

"You should spend some time practicing with that weapon so you know how it works and what to expect from firing it. Akata can set you up with a target to shoot." Ethan steered me toward the viewscreen room.

Staring at my hands, I didn't know what to think or feel. "What if I hurt somebody?"

Ethan took my hand in both of his. "Emma, I don't want you to hurt anyone. I don't think you're the kind of person who can rebound from that. But I also don't want you to get hurt. Sometimes, you wind up having to make a choice. That choice is between you and someone else."

He let go to nudge under my chin so I met his gaze. "If you ever have to make a choice between anyone and yourself, I want you to choose yourself. Even if the other person is me. I said it before, and I meant it. Sometimes, it's about survival, and that's not selfish."

My eyes itched with tears. I nodded even though I knew I couldn't do what he wanted. If I had to choose between Ethan and myself, I'd always choose Ethan. He had so much more to offer the universe than I did. Anyone could do math. Only Ethan could be Ethan.

"Good." He wrapped his arms around me and held me while I cried. Again.

CHAPTER 19

Hours later, I stood in the airlock hallway, covered in my coral suit and waiting for Akata to dock with the facility. The suit held my new gun at my hip with enough of the grip showing for me to draw it. I hadn't practiced much with it yet, but Ethan didn't think I needed to for our first scouting run.

The less time I spent practicing with it, the less chance I ever had to shoot someone.

We planned to explore as much as possible and evacuate as many times as necessary until I could find a way to disable the whole place or activate the wormhole in reverse. Ethan would stick with me while we all split up to investigate unknown hallways.

The ship rolled sideways and static crowded my vision. I noticed the nausea didn't seem as sharp as the last time we'd stopped. That didn't matter, though.

As soon as the airlock opened, we rushed across to the red glow of the facility. The guys split into two pairs at the first intersection. Mendez and Ethan parted at the next intersection. I jogged behind Ethan, too out of breath to tell him he ran too fast. When he stopped, I leaned against the wall and gasped to suck in air.

"You used to be able to keep up with me," Ethan said as he peered down a crossing hallway. He breathed normally, like we'd strolled at a leisurely pace.

"You weren't a Marine," I puffed.

"We didn't run that far." He nodded for us to turn to the left and set a much slower pace.

I followed him without answering, dragging my coral-covered fingertips across the smooth wall. An unexpected change in the scraping noise I made caught my attention. I stopped and took a closer look.

As I bent and peered at an extra seam, the metal punched outward. I turned my head enough to take the blow on my cheek. My vision exploded with white sparks. Pain chased them. Green light disoriented me. The world spun and slid.

Everything took a long time to stop whirling. I looked up and saw Ethan kicking a robot in front of me. He threw his shoulder into it and shoved the thing like a linebacker defending his end zone.

I lay on the floor. The wall had an unexpected hole with a panel raised above it on hydraulic arms. For some unknown reason, I sat up and crawled into the hole. In the moment, it seemed like a good idea. Like I could learn something useful, and the unexpected opportunity needed seizing.

As I crawled inside, I thought the hole more suited the term "alcove." It seemed about the right size to hold the robot Ethan faced. In the back, a cord with a three-prong plug hung from the center of the wall. Slim rods perched parallel to the floor in a number of spots along the sides, and I suspected they could extend and retract. Maybe they held the robot in place.

Arms on the sides lowered with a mechanical hum. My head was still fuzzy, which meant it took until the door blocked any hope of escape before I realized my situation.

"Ethan!"

The door snapped into place, cutting off the light. I sat in the dark. Sharp stabs of panic cleared my head. I pounded on the door with my coral-covered fists.

Everything shuddered. Mechanical things whirred. I rode the floor downward. The walls moved with me, so the entire alcove slid down. The movement stopped with a clunk and jiggle. Showing me exactly how I took a blow to the head, the door punched out two inches and slid up.

I scrambled out, toward dim white light.

When my vision cleared, I sat in a square room with one convex wall. Blue-white light came from the far end. I didn't understand this until I scrambled to my feet and trotted toward the light. A gap in the odd wall let me step into a sphere made of screens.

Each screen showed part of the facility with higher resolution than any monitor I'd ever seen. On one, Ethan wrestled with that robot. Nash picked up the crowbar they'd lost on our last foray and pried open a panel. Baldwin fired his rifle down a hallway. Mendez ran from one image to another with a robot trundling behind him at high speed.

Did this room monitor or control? I saw no keyboard or other input device, so I commanded the coral off my hand and tapped the nearest screen. Over the image of Ethan, a white rectangle with twelve lines of symbols appeared. It reminded me of a context menu, but I couldn't read it.

Lines and triangles formed every symbol, each with a different arrangement to make a different pattern. They reminded me of hieroglyphics, except with fewer elements. No birds or people, just lines and triangles.

English probably looked like lines, triangles, and circles to people who couldn't read it. I knew kids who felt that way about math.

"Akata, do you understand any of this writing?"

"I have no experience with any written language."

I hesitated to choose any of the options. For all I knew, the menu let an operator switch the robots from stun to lethal. Of course, if they did, considering their interest in keeping everybody alive, that seemed like an option they'd put low on the list. A last resort with multiple confirmations, most likely.

At worst, I figured I could open the menu and tap the same option again. I picked the first one on the list.

The menu disappeared. I heard grunting and the clang of metal on metal.

"Cog?" Though he focused on the robot, Ethan twisted to check on me. "Where are you?"

Audio. I tapped for the menu again and chose the first option again. The audio feed stopped. Go me, I'd learned something.

The second, third, and fourth menu options changed the angle of the image, probably by switching to different cameras. This facility had a ridiculous number of cameras. I hadn't noticed any of them, so I wondered what they looked like.

Finally, with the fifth option, the robot stopped struggling. Ethan stepped back, checking behind him. I had to make sure, so I chose it again. The robot moved, so I turned it off again.

I shut down the other robots chasing the guys. Finding a system-wide shutdown option would've been ideal, but at least four of them wouldn't chase us anymore.

Ethan attracted my attention by kicking his robot. Nothing happened. He twisted and moved his mouth like he called for me.

"I need one of those microphone and earbud things they have."

"They have extras. When you return to the ship, I will make certain you acquire one."

Extras. They had extra Earth-based equipment. Akata wanted to give me gear from a dead man. Gross. Necessary, but gross.

Mendez encountered another robot, so I shut it down. He stopped running to prod the robot.

The floor rocked. All four men stumbled and braced against the walls.

"Sentinels," Akata said. "They have activated. Their

attacks will target sections of the station with the goal of disrupting organics without damaging them. The weapons are quite interesting in function. I am fortunate they do not recognize me as an organic to disrupt. I believe the consequences would be severe for my systems if that changed."

"That's not ominous or anything," I mumbled.

"Thus far, my outer shell and the force field generated by it have shielded me. I believe I register as dead organic material instead of living."

"But you're not invisible, right? They could see you on cameras?"

"This is correct. I have no stealth capabilities."

The lack of an operator for the screens, combined with this new information, led me to conclude the facility ran on automation. Maybe someone came once in a while to bring more people across. The rest of the time, nothing so far suggested anything as complex as a full AI managing everything.

Which left algorithms. I understood algorithms.

"Okay. At the core of all computer code is math. Math is a universal language. I should be able to find something simple and basic that can act as a primer for at least some part of how the systems are controlled. Somewhere. Step one— what can this suite do besides monitor cameras and issue commands to robots?"

"We do not have that information."

"Yet. We don't have that information yet." I tapped a screen showing an empty hallway and tried every menu option to see what happened. One controlled a bank of white lights in the hallway. Where did the lights come from? I hadn't seen any on the ceilings or walls. Another option operated a robot alcove door.

"Can you figure out the symbols based upon what these options do?"

"We can work on deciphering it during your next sleep cycle."

Something to look forward to, because I enjoyed cryptography and logic puzzles. Of course, if we succeeded beyond my expectations today, I might never have to work on any of it.

The rest of the menu options had no obvious effect on the hallway. I made sure to undo each tap in case I'd turned on pressure-sensitive poison gas nozzles or worse. As a final test, I tapped each screen to check the menus. Each showed the same list.

By the time I decided to find an exit, the guys had converged. Ethan seemed animated with his distress. He thought he'd lost me.

"I'm going to guess you don't know how to get here other than through that robot alcove I have no idea how to control aside from the door."

"Correct."

Great. I turned on the audio for the screen showing all the guys, figuring they'd make a plan to find me. If I knew it, I could do my part to make that work faster.

Several screens showed them from multiple angles, so I could see all their faces.

"I have no idea," Ethan grumbled. He rubbed his face. "We can run a search pattern starting at the last place I saw her."

Nash crossed his arms. "Harper, maybe this ain't the best time, what with the sentinels active and all, but there's something I need to tell you about your sister."

"You're right." Ethan's eyes narrowed. "This isn't the best time."

"Naw, man, it's not about her being a pretty girl." Nash raised his hands in surrender. "She has a problem. And you're not seeing it."

"I know she has a problem. It's the same problem we all had when we got here."

Nash shook his head. "This is something else."

I didn't know what Nash had to say, but I needed to

hear it. I stood, rooted to the spot, wishing he'd hurry up and explain.

The station rocked again. Ethan picked a direction and they jogged that way. The cameras followed them, and so did the audio pickups.

"Back in high school, my junior year, we had six kids pass out in gym class in a span of three weeks. Just boom, on the floor, and taken away by an ambulance. After the sixth one, a guy, we all got to take a week of health class instead of gym. They talked about food, nutrition, and eating disorders. We had a bigass test on that stuff, and it counted for a lot of our grade."

My heart pounded in my throat. "No," I whispered.

"I been watching Emma since she showed up. I bet she'd be pretty with some meat on her bones, but all she is, it's bones. She's a walking pile of sticks, and that ain't normal."

"I know that," Ethan snapped. "I can see it. She's too thin and she thinks she's gross. I figure—"

"Shut up, Harper. This is serious." Nash smacked Ethan's shoulder. "I been watching her, and Akata helped me go over some of what I've seen. I'd bet serious money on her being bulimic."

My stomach churned and my heart raced. He used the "b" word. Nobody used that word. I didn't have a problem. I just needed help to calm down sometimes. Like now. If I could purge now, everything would be fine.

"I don't know what that means," Ethan said.

"Day-umn," Baldwin said.

Mendez raised his brow. "That's the one where they eat and puke it up, right?"

"Yeah. I thought maybe she was anorexic, because I could see her bones, but then I watched her eat. There's woman who likes food. When Mendez listed what was in the noodle bowl, she made this face at the word 'fat' that was so full of disgust, it was crazy. Her stomach growls and she says she ain't hungry. The whites of her eyes are yellowish. She's weak. Can't even lift a rifle, and these things ain't that heavy. She sleeps a lot. She's probably passed out or zoned out lots of times without realizing it. I think she's obsessed with fat and can't see past some messed-up idea of herself to what she really looks like. Another few months or maybe a year of doing that, and she'll kill herself."

They jogged in silence. I wanted to curl up and die.

"I..." Ethan raked a hand through his short hair. "I have no idea what to do about that."

Nash shrugged. "Yeah, I don't either. They told us to tell a teacher if we saw the symptoms in somebody. But there's something else too."

I switched off the audio with a shaking hand and fled the room as the facility rocked again.

CHAPTER 20

I found a toilet. Outside the screens room, I discovered living quarters. Twelve rooms each housed two bare twin-size beds on metal frames, two metal desks, two closets, and two metal chairs. Two had random clothing and broken electronics on the floor, like the previous occupants had packed with haste and evacuated.

They looked like the Bentley dorm rooms I'd toured with Dad for spring break.

Worst spring break ever, by the way. All my friends had gone to beaches or forest cabins as adult-free groups while I'd flown with my parents to Massachusetts to see my inevitable doom. When we all compared pictures at home, everyone else had sand, surf, hiking, bikinis, flowers, hot cocoa, beer, and fun. Mine...

Maybe I hadn't given Bentley a chance. Once I had an accounting degree, I could go on to something else. Accounting at least involved numbers, unlike a lot of other options. The mass transit system around Boston meant I could rove across the area and do all kinds of things.

If I tried, I thought I could find a professor at MIT who'd help me. They cared about skill.

Then nothing Nash said would matter, and everything would be fine.

I stared at the metal toilet inside a stall in the

communal bathroom. It had some subtle design differences from the ones I knew, but overall seemed the same. The nearby sinks had no water, so the toilets wouldn't work either. That oatmeal clung to my gut, spreading the fat from my last meal across my body. Of course, it had been long enough that I didn't think purging would do me any good anymore. Dry heaving sucked. I needed exercise.

Nash didn't know anything. I wasn't a pile of sticks. I was a gross, freakish pile of fat. I wore a size four! Someday, when I got rid of all the dark goo inside me, I'd fit into a zero.

My feet shuffled me close to the toilet.

"Your body does not require the use of this type of device at this time. Even if it did, this one is non-functional."

Akata's voice startled me. She'd been silent long enough for me to forget about her.

The station rocked and I bounced against the stall. I backed out despite a desire to touch the bowl. Groping for some excuse to linger, I thought of the people who'd built the facility.

"Why would the people here have toilets like the ones we use on Earth?"

"The internal workings may differ considerably from the devices you know."

"Suggesting they have similar anatomy to us, and came up with the same overall idea for that purpose."

"Some functionalities are rather universal."

Like doors and windows. Square structures. Chairs. Screens. I nodded. "Sure." These people, whoever they were and whatever they wanted, unnerved me. They built a facility capable of dragging people across the universe for unknown reasons, then abandoned it to automated functions. If someone had defeated the people, why leave the facility intact?

"This place is messed up." I fled the bathroom and continued through the living quarters. Once I found the way out and mapped it with Akata's help, I could find it again if I wanted.

I didn't believe a word Nash had said. He was wrong, flat wrong. Ethan would see that. So would Mendez. Not that I cared what Mendez thought, but he'd see it.

At the end of the hall, I stopped and peered in both directions of a T intersection. Each ran straight along the wall forever. Unlike the living area, where white lights made everything seem almost normal, the hallway had red lights.

Maybe the red lights somehow used less power, or cost less to build and replace. Thinking about how much work it would take to replace every light bulb in the facility distracted me from everything. Checking the ceiling, I didn't see white lights in the new hallway, so maybe it didn't have any. Then again, I couldn't see the red bulbs either.

"Which direction should I go?"

"Look for a way to move from one level to another. You descended to reach this section, so you require a method to ascend."

"Putting elevators or ladders near living quarters makes sense. It's what I did in all my designs." I picked left for no reason.

Ten steps down the hall, Akata said, "Another ship has entered the nearby space. I believe it did so a few minutes ago and I did not notice it on the other side of the facility."

Panic surged through me. My whole body shivered. Andy the wolfman had come for me. "Is it a lepiku ship?"

"Negative. Registering the sentinels adjusting weapon arrays toward me. I believe I have been detected."

Worse, someone had come for Akata. "Get out of here! If they fire, you don't know what'll happen."

"Before I leave the vicinity, you must remove the coral armor. Otherwise, it will die on your body and immobilize you." Sometimes, she used way too many words to say things.

"Come back for us. Please."

"I will," Akata said as the coral slid off my skin to form a thick, oozing puddle on the floor.

The interface disconnected. Alone and unprotected, I

hugged myself. I had to find Ethan and the guys without knowing where to look. The gun surfaced in the pile. I picked it up.

At school, they always said if you got lost, stay where you are, or only wander a short distance to find an authority figure, like a cop or a mall employee. The guys, though, had never come to this level. If they hadn't found it before, they wouldn't find it now either. Like Akata said, I needed to find a way up to the next level.

Crackling attracted my attention. The coral on the floor darkened and shuddered. Akata had either escaped or died. We officially had no way off the facility except the wormhole. I prayed for Akata to have escaped. She would come back.

Fifty or sixty feet farther down the hallway, a bright light flared. I froze. What would I do if a robot came for me?

Duh, I'd head for the screen room and turn it off.

The light came from a door of some kind. A person-shaped silhouette grew until a matching creature stepped through the doorway. He or she, or it—whatever—turned and walked toward me. They stopped, probably because they saw me.

A male-sounding voice came from that direction, asking a question in a language I didn't know.

I gulped and answered. "Sorry, I don't understand."

The creature approached. As he neared, I noted his navy, form-fitting suit with thick boots. Short, spiky black hair stood out against his bright blue skin. Instead of ears, he had two foot-long antennae sticking behind his head. Otherwise, he seemed human.

He spoke again, this time without a question.

Hoping body language would work with this guy, I held up my hand and flashed him a sheepish smile.

Nodding to himself, he stuck a hand in a pocket, withdrew a slim device shaped like an electric shaver, and pointed it at me. He pointed at me with his finger, then at the hallway behind me.

His distrust didn't surprise me. If I came across a strange alien on my facility, I'd pull a weapon too.

Wait. I had a weapon in my hand. He had a weapon in his hand. Static flickered on the edges of my vision. I thought my heart might explode out of my chest.

He said something else, and it sounded annoyed. When I did nothing, he pressed a button on his handheld device. Blue crackles of energy poured out and slammed me to the floor. My body spasmed and I couldn't think. Aching pain spread from the base of my neck to the tips of my fingers and toes.

The alien guy strolled to my feet and looked down at me. He smirked and pushed the button again. Everything stopped.

I gasped for breath. Nothing worked, not even my pinky toes. Lying limp on the floor, watched him grab my foot.

He kicked away the gun, dragged me through a new door, and tossed me into a bare metal room. My head hit the wall, making me see static again. I crumpled into a heap. The door clanged shut like a death knell.

Unable to move, I closed my eyes inside my four-foot-cube jail cell and refused to cry. Not this time.

Not for him.

CHAPTER 21

Feeling returned to my limbs inch by inch. I lay in a pile, aching and numb at the same time.

I'd had a gun and didn't use it. The weapon in my hand could've saved me from this situation, but I couldn't make myself use it. Now I had no weapon, no Akata coral armor, no Ethan, no nothing. No hope.

My brain decided I needed worse, so it replayed everything Nash had said.

Bulimia. I knew the word and what it meant. People with it ate a ton, bingeing on ice cream or other stuff, then either barfed it back up or exercised a lot. I didn't do that. I never binged. One slice of cheesecake didn't count as a binge, it counted as a serving. And so what if I ate a whole pint of ice cream, so long as I didn't digest it?

The gym teachers all said I did a great job in class. They would know if someone over-exercised. Besides, my workouts followed a video meant for daily use. Maybe I sometimes did it twice or three times, but only when I'd had cheesecake or a strawberry shake. Normal people did extra exercise when they had a treat.

I didn't have a problem.

The ache in my head lessened. I shifted until I lay flat on my back. As I moved, my vision clouded with static and cleared twice.

Wanting to lose weight didn't cause the static. No matter what Nash thought, he didn't know everything. The static happened when I got stressed. Or hungry. I ate when I got hungry. Obviously, my prison prevented me from eating anytime soon. Not that I wanted to eat. Between noodle bowl, devil's food oatmeal, and waffle dreams...

I salivated. My stomach growled. That last meal seemed forever ago. I needed water. No, tea. Water was boring. Tea had flavor, and I usually added skim milk. And honey. Sometimes, we didn't have skim milk, so I used the heavy cream and dunked sandwich cookies in it. The whole thing tasted at least as good as Akata's waffles.

Admittedly, the coming back up part sucked, but going down, I died and went to heaven. That part made the purging worthwhile. How much it calmed me made it worthwhile. Everything made it worthwhile.

Someday I'd reach size zero like all my favorite models and actresses. Everyone would like me. Nothing bad would happen anymore. I could stop tasting bile all the time.

I really did hate the taste of bile. It made my eyes water and my nose sting. If I purged twice in one day, it gave me a headache, and I hated that too. Nothing tasted good for over an hour after purging, though that helped me not eat for a while, so it served a purpose.

I didn't have a problem.

Nash just wanted to get into my pants, like every other guy. He figured he could rescue me or something, like every other guy.

Memories reared. I didn't want them. Tiffany's boyfriend stuck his hand up my skirt and everyone laughed. Bridget's boyfriend groped me as he passed in English class and no one saw it. Andy dragged me onto a bed and yanked down my underwear—

No. I didn't want to think about that stuff. Finding a way out of this box needed to take priority. If I could move, I could escape, with or without a gun.

Staring at the ceiling with my thoughts derailed, I noticed a shiny spot in the corner. Cameras. This place had cameras everywhere. Like the girls' locker room at school. Last September, Madison and I found three in the showers. We'd ripped them down and stomped on them instead of reporting them. Deep down, I think neither of us had wanted anyone else to see our gross, fat bodies.

Knowing that alien guy watched me gave me shivers down my spine. He would see every move I made. As soon as I got to my feet, he'd know I could. So I needed to play weak. If I feigned weakness well enough, he might come to see me and try to talk again. Or he could come to feed me.

I imagined him bringing a tray. I'd lurch to my feet, flip the tray in his face, and rush him. We'd fall through the door and I'd steal his zappy-taser-thing and my gun so he couldn't zap me again. Then I'd run down the hall and find the stairs, find the guys, and let them beat up the alien and we would steal his ship.

In addition, I'd shrink two sizes, Baldwin would turn into a unicorn, and a battalion of space Marines would escort us home.

The guys might keep him occupied for a little while. They knew how to deal with the robots well enough that he might have to control them manually. His distraction might let me explore my prison enough to find a weakness or a way out.

On the other hand, if I distracted him, the guys would have more time to find me. Except I already knew they had no idea about this section of the facility. They wouldn't find me.

I had to take a chance that the guys kept him busy.

Lifting my head took more effort than I expected. Static crinkled around the edges of my vision. I rested. Nash's words rumbled in my ears again, telling Ethan I probably passed out sometimes.

The static had almost wrecked my car. I had no idea how bad the crash could've been. It might've killed all of us.

Inertia could've dragged us off the road to hit pedestrians. Flying glass could've hurt people.

My heart raced as I realized how close I'd come to death. Because my vision clouded with static.

How long had it been happening? I remembered waking up one November morning when the heat hadn't kicked on yet. I'd had to pee or I would've stayed under the covers. The chill in the house had made me shiver so hard my teeth chattered. Sitting on the frosty toilet seat, static had scared the crap out of me for the first time.

The second time had been about a month later, then they grew more frequent. Did that first one really count? Shying away from the math, I decided to call it six months.

My first time purging had happened a few days after that time when… It was November of my junior year. I'd tried it once to see if it worked. That first time, I hadn't known how to do it. Learning how not to scrape my throat with my fingernail had taken practice. Handling the burning in my chest had taken practice.

I didn't have a problem.

Did I?

Three months ago, I'd only purged once a week or so. As long as I kept my nose in a book and stayed away from my friends, I never faced temptation. They always wanted me to go out and sit in cafes. We watched people walk by and mocked them.

Why did we do that?

I remembered watching one of my neighbors, a girl with thick thighs and short hair. She'd smiled with true joy as she passed us, laughing with a friend. How did a person feel that good when they had so much cellulite? Her laughter confused me, even now, because it had seemed so genuine.

We'd muttered and giggled between us about thunder thighs and sausage fingers. But I hadn't felt happy about that. Not like the girl had seemed. None of us had smiled, not for real. Joy hadn't prompted our giggles. The episode had made my stomach queasy, and I remembered purging my tea to calm it.

The tea had come up easier than food. Mass quantities of liquid didn't burn.

Did I have a problem? Did other people know what to expect when they barfed? Why did it calm me to do that? Why did I even start? That first time, I'd cried and wanted to die. So I did it again? What kind of person did that?

Nash was a boy, he didn't know anything.

But what if he did know things? What if he knew things about this?

What if Nash knew better than me about this one thing?

What if, when Ethan said I looked gaunt, he told the truth?

I thought about what I'd eaten over the last week before coming through the wormhole.

One egg for breakfast every day. Except for Monday and Thursday. I'd added salt. Cheese. Smashed cereal. Orange juice. A banana.

On Monday and Thursday, I'd purged after breakfast because the buffet spread in the school cafeteria had turned me into a fat cow.

For lunch, diet soda, an apple, and one slice of bread from a sandwich. Except for Saturday, Sunday, Tuesday, and Friday, when I'd eaten at the trough. Mom always wanted dessert on the weekends, after every meal. She loved chocolates, lemon cakes and cookies, and biscuits with butter and jam. My thighs swelled just thinking about them.

Mom made the biscuits from scratch. Melted butter sizzled on the baking stone, filling the kitchen with the most amazing aroma. I loved that smell. That smell said Mom cared and I got to eat something delicious. We slathered the fluffy nuggets with more butter and jam from the farmer's market.

Then I left the kitchen for the third floor. As soon as I lost the scent, I realized what I'd done. Visions of that butter swimming in my veins had made me purge. The stream of barely digested food destroyed the pleasure of eating it in the first place, so the next time, I did sit-ups until I dropped to atone instead.

Oh God, I had a problem.

CHAPTER 22

My heart raced again. I thought my chest might explode. What would I do? How would I calm down if I never purged again? How would I ever reach a size zero?

How would I get the stupid door open so any of these things mattered?

Right. Focus. I needed to focus on the immediate problem so I could find answers to the other problems. Taking one step at a time worked. When I cleaned things, I always started with one part, then moved to the next, and things got done. The laundry couldn't go through the dryer until I washed it, after all.

Ignoring the idea of cameras, I brushed my hand along the floor and the wall. Both felt smooth and flat. I rapped my knuckles against each. The floor sounded solid and felt like steel. The wall seemed plasticky. Seams showed me the floor had several plates while the walls didn't.

In my possession, I had my boots and clothes, several broken fingernails, and a wad of red curls. The second two wouldn't help me accomplish much.

For the first time, I took a closer look at my Akata-provided clothes. My blush pink outfit had no zippers, snaps, buttons, ties, or elastic. The material fit my body without any of those things. Akata applied and removed it at need. Except now, of course.

I murmured a prayed for Akata. She had escaped. I knew it.

That didn't help me, though, because I had nothing to work with. My fingers wouldn't fit into those seams, and it had no loose sections. Scrapes too shallow to matter marred the steel. I saw no signs of rust or corrosion.

Escaping from this room would take a different kind of effort. I could try enacting the non-ridiculous parts of my earlier fantasy, except I doubted I had the strength to accomplish it.

That left the cameras.

What if the alien guy had no idea what I could accomplish? What if I could make him think I had a way to open the door or damage a panel?

If only I'd been a drama nerd.

Then again, hadn't I acted for my parents all this time? Every day, I smiled and pretended my grades came from a lack of brains on my part. I didn't want them to know about my dreams. If they didn't know, they couldn't use it against me.

One time, around age seven, I told my dad I wanted to make rockets. He'd patted me on the head and given me an antique adding machine.

"That's nice, Sweetie. You're going to be an accountant, like Daddy. That's better than building rockets."

Sure, Dad. Performing basic math functions and keeping track of tax laws is so much better than building machines to take people to the stars. I'd lived that lie for eleven years.

I sat up. Static fringed the edges of my vision. When I sat still, it faded. Given the room's emptiness, I thought the corner would work best. I crawled to the one closest to the door and used my body to block my hands. Facing the corner, I leaned my head and side against one wall, and used my legs to form as much of a barrier as I could against the other.

Hoping he thought I had some wild ability to do something with nothing, I moved my hands in the bottom corner. I made sure to move my arms too. From the outside, I thought it would appear that I had some device or parts I might use to cut through the wall. For good measure, I alternated my facial expressions between a frustrated frown, a grin of success, and my tongue sticking out like I did when I soldered delicate electronics.

Time passed so slow it might as well had stood still. I got the feeling the alien guy didn't buy my act.

Then the door burst open. He shouted and pointed his taser-thing at me. When he waved for me to move, I blubbered like I'd been caught and scrambled to my feet.

He bent to peer at the corner. I rushed around him. He half-turned. I shoved him at the corner. He squawked. I dove through the door. Before he could get back to his feet, I turned, slammed it shut, flipped a switch that I hoped locked it, and ran.

I sprinted as fast as my legs could carry me to reach the screens room. If the alien had caught the guys, I needed to know before I ran across the entire station trying to find them.

In the distance, I heard a boom echo down the tunnel. Alien guy had broken free of the little prison room. Where would he go? Probably the screens room to find me. I needed to hide.

Picking one of the bedrooms at random, I darted inside and ducked into the empty closet. I found the door open, so I left it that way and made myself as small as I could in the darkness of the back corner. Every fiber of my being worked on catching my breath and staying quiet. Alien guy would pass, reach the screens room, and watch for me.

I'd escaped from one prison to drop myself into another one.

Boots hurried past, clomping on the metal floor. While I could still hear his boots growing more distant, I pushed the accordion-style closet door closer to shut. The more space I had, the easier I could breathe.

The screens had shown the guys when I reached them.

Considering how many cameras this place had to have, that meant the screens targeted movement. I stayed still.

After a long time that probably only covered a few minutes, the meager light from the hallway let me notice odd-shaped things scattered on the floor around me, and under my butt. I'd picked one of the rooms with broken things. Keeping my movements small and slow, I patted each lump to try to find something useful.

Everything felt like plastic or cloth. As far as I could imagine, cloth wouldn't help me. The plastic things, though, had rough edges. That kind of sharpness could cut things.

What would I cut? The blue-skin alien? I couldn't even raise a gun to threaten him when he already threatened me. Even if I could overcome that, I didn't have the strength to use any of these things to damage a teddy bear, let alone flesh.

One object seemed potentially useful. Between an exploration of its shape with my fingers and the minimal light, I thought I'd found a screwdriver shank with no handle. One end had a flat edge, the other felt ragged. In the center, it had a weird, bumpy ridge I'd have to see in better light to interpret.

Nothing else on the floor seemed useful. Even if I couldn't get a good grip on this thing, or couldn't find any screws, at least I had something that could function like a lever or cutting edge. Since I couldn't leave the closet without risking discovery, I turned my attention to the side wall behind the door.

To cut down on noise, I ran my fingertips over the wall first and found a seam. This wall felt like the plasticky wall in that prison room. The screwdriver blade fit into the seam much better than my finger. I took my time prying it open.

Tiny things flew at my face as I chipped through some kind of sealant different from gray coral. Some landed in my mouth. It tasted like sawdust. I wiped off my tongue and thought about barfing this stuff up. Ingesting a substance used to hold together pieces of a space station sounded worse than eating fat. A lot worse.

Purging now, though, would either leave me sitting in a stinking pile of vomit or reveal me because it triggered the motion sensors. Which meant no barfing for me. Not now.

Not ever again? Maybe? How much fixing did I need? How did I fix it at all? Nash and Ethan had no ideas. Maybe Baldwin or Mendez would think of something.

The panel separated. If I ever built a space station, I wouldn't allow this kind of shoddy work. We'd use rivets with real sealant, or that gray coral stuff. Even in the closets. Parts needed to stay together or the whole thing collapsed.

I shifted the panel to rest against the back wall, hoping the darkness kept the minor movement from attracting camera attention.

It occurred to me that the living quarters might have actual privacy, but I couldn't take that chance. Better to assume a camera than to get caught.

The revealed panel had no helpful lights. Though I knew it was a bad idea, I stuck my hand into it. My fingers touched irregular surfaces, so I knew I'd found something besides another wall. Destroying things without knowing anything about them would cause problems when we tried to use the wormhole device later.

Because we'd use that device later. This alien jerk wouldn't stop me. I had to think, but I didn't have to give up.

I wouldn't give up. Not on Ethan, not on Mendez, Nash, and Baldwin. And not on myself. Not anymore.

CHAPTER 23

Poking the stuff inside the panel got me nowhere. I tried to imagine what systems might run alongside the living quarters and came up with too many options, most of them critical. When I did my next ship design, I decided I'd put critical life support components next to the crew quarters. The choice made a lot of sense.

Also, I had nothing else to think about. Every option that came to mind resulted in a high probability of me dead or back in a box. Alien guy wouldn't fall for the same trick twice.

While I sat, crafting a ship design in my head, I heard boots clomping from the screen room toward me. No one else had traveled in the other direction, so alien guy had come out for some reason. I stilled and kept my breathing quiet.

He moved at a brisk pace, faster than walking and slower than running. The sound paused close to my room, and the pause lasted forever times two. Then he moved on, heading away from the screens room and away from me. His boots clomped into the distance, too far for me to hear anymore.

I had one chance. Maybe he'd return in five hours, or maybe five minutes. Either way, I didn't know if I'd get another chance.

Unconcerned with the noise I made, I gripped my screwdriver and scrambled out of the closet. I sprinted to the screens room. Alien guy had left. He wouldn't see me.

Ethan and the guys lay inside a small room like my prison. It looked like the same box Akata had shown me, the one the robots had herded them to on their first visit. Ethan sat on his knees, shaking his head in his hands. The others stirred enough to know they all lived. I guessed the robots had stunned and dumped them.

Another screen showed the alien guy striding through the station, his taser-thing in hand. I saw no sign of my gun, either on his person or in the screens room. Maybe he'd locked it up.

He climbed a set of narrow stairs. I needed to find them. As the screen shifted to show his progress through the station, I noticed tiny black things left in his wake. Somehow, he left a crumb trail for me to follow.

Thank goodness, because the changing camera angles made his path hard to track. Knowing I didn't need to pay so much attention to his progress, I gave some thought to how I would follow him without him seeing me.

Cameras needed power, but I had no idea how to target them. Screens also needed power. When I'd found the screen room, I came through the back. Though I hadn't seen the cables, I hadn't looked for them either.

I ducked behind the screens and wished I had a flashlight. My heart pounded, expecting alien guy to change his mind and come back. Would he catch me in here? Did the screen room have cameras? Probably not, or the person monitoring the station would wind up watching himself all the time.

Running my hands over the backs of the screens, I discovered wires running across the backs. They merged into the black wires I'd found elsewhere on the station. On the backs of the screens closest to the ceiling, I saw the black wires dive into a hole in the screen housing.

Since I couldn't reach it, I raised my screwdriver and thought about smashing all the screens. Destruction on that scale seemed likely to get me caught. Alien guy would step inside the room, see all the smashed glass, and run out. He'd probably return to the guys, because that made the most sense.

I suspected my screwdriver could cut the wires. Alternatively, I could rip them out of the screens. In that case, alien guy might take a half a minute to puzzle over the situation before dashing out to apprehend me. Half a minute might mean all the difference to me.

Before doing that, I stepped into the screen section again and disabled as many robots as I could. We needed to roam as freely as possible. If alien guy had a remote for them, we'd have to suck it up and deal with that.

That done, I circled them again and hacked at wires with my screwdriver. In the light, I saw the shank's middle section allowed the whole thing to fold and swap the blade for other shapes. The design interested me, but I had other things to do.

Hacking through the wires didn't work. The screwdriver wasn't sharp enough to cut the wires inside the black stuff. I grabbed a wire, wrapped it around the shank, and used both hands to yank with all my strength. On the third try, it ripped out of the screen. Only twenty-nine more to go. Ethan could've done two at a time.

I took deep breaths and moved from screen to screen, starting with the lowest and working my way to the top row. Once I reached the top row, I had to give up. I lacked the strength and height. Twenty screens out of commission would have to suffice.

Checking from the other side, I noticed the screens had screws on the bottom. Of course they did. I whipped through removing a bunch of screws and found an easier way to disconnect the wires. For good measure, I replaced the bottom. The time it had taken to use this method seemed similar to the time for ripping them out from the back, so I attacked the rest.

As I did so, I saw the alien guy on one of the remaining screens. He kept walking, and I couldn't tell if he'd reached his destination yet or not. I worked as fast as I could.

The last screen flickered off with an image of him walking down a set of stairs. I put one screw back to hold the bottom together, then I fled the room for the bedroom I'd used before. Ten seconds after I hid behind the door, I heard his boots echoing down the hall toward me. He moved at the same brisk pace as before.

Part of me wanted to leap out and tackle him. I could take the taser-thingy and use it on him. He seemed in better shape than me, though, so I doubted it would go like I wanted.

The shank had a blade, but I'd already proven I couldn't use it. I needed to reach Ethan and the guys. They could use it.

Alien guy took forever to pass me without stopping. His footfalls kept moving, then something muffled them in a different way. I peeked out of the door and saw no sign of him. Across the hall, I thought that bedroom door had been open more. If he'd ducked into a room, he'd given me the best chance to flee I thought I'd get.

Running on my toes, I tried not to make any noise. Every scuff of my boots echoed at a zillion decibels, but he didn't reappear before I turned the corner. I gasped for breath from the close call as much as the running.

Down the hall, I saw the pile of dead coral and headed toward it. The goo had spread across the hallway, covering it from one wall to the other with a thin pile of black ash-like muck mixed with the red sticks the guys used as currency.

Alien guy had stepped in it and left a bootprint, then tracked it through the station. That explained the black specks.

I scooped up a handful of the sticks and stuffed them into my pocket for no reason other than the perception they had value to someone. Earth scientists might want to analyze them, at least.

Even better, armed with dead space coral, Ethan and I could try to get a meeting with NASA people. We could get into programs or something. And if the wormhole option didn't work, we used them as money with the greenies. Win-win.

The wormhole option would work. We'd all go home. I'd get help. Ethan would punch Dad in the face.

I followed the smudges of ash like my life depended on it. They took me up a narrow flight of stairs for two levels, then down a hallway. The tracks faded to nothing. Determined to find the guys, I ran down the hallway and peered around every corner.

In front of a door, I found a deactivated robot. The thing and its tank-like treads blocked the door, no matter which way it opened. Since it did nothing, though, I stepped onto the left tread and climbed around it to reach the door handle.

By now, alien guy had figured out that I ran amok. Would he try to reconnect the screens or guess my goal and come running? No way to know until either the robot reactivated or he turned a corner and zapped me.

I found a switch that sounded like a lock and tried to open the door. The bottom whacked into the treads, because of course it opened outward.

"Ethan!" I shouted through a tiny crack between the door and wall.

"Emma?" I recognized Baldwin's lilt.

"Baldwin, there's a robot in front of the door. I deactivated it, but it's too heavy for me to move."

"That blue-skin guy?"

"He could show up any second."

Baldwin paused for a moment. "Okay. Others are tased. Get out of the way."

I scrambled off the robot and stood well clear. Something, I assumed Baldwin, thumped against the door. The door banged against the robot, shifting it a millimeter.

The robot's treads shrieked against the metal floor. Alien guy would hear it from across the station and come running.

If I didn't find a place to hide, he'd tase me.

Baldwin slammed into the door again and shoved the robot another millimeter or two with another piercing squeal.

Checking the hallway, I found another outward-opening door with a lock on the outside. No way did I want to put myself into that kind of a prison on purpose. The bedroom had worked for me because I could get myself out when I wanted. This ran too much risk of the alien guy locking the door on me.

The robot screeched again.

"Emma. Hide."

I gulped and nodded. "I have a screwdriver." Why did I say that? No idea.

"Really? Give it here." Baldwin had a wide enough opening for me to pass it through. He met my gaze with one eye. "You're doing great. Won't leave without you."

Covering my mouth so I could suppress a surge of some weird feeling I couldn't place that made me want to cry, I backed away from the door and ran for the other room. Baldwin kept throwing himself at the door. I pulled my door almost shut, leaving it open a crack.

Alien guy sprinted into view. He ran to the other door and stuck his hand into the room. Whatever happened, he howled and snatched back his hand. I saw something dark, maybe blood. He panted and staggered backward, then ran.

The robot screeched across the floor again. The next time, it shrieked for at least two seconds. Baldwin and Nash spilled out of the room together. Nash held the taser-thingy, Baldwin had the screwdriver. They gave each other a high-five.

CHAPTER 24

Not sure what I felt, I burst out of the room and hugged Nash. "I'm sorry, you were right and I didn't mean to shout or anything I just couldn't believe it but the things you said made me think and you were right and I have a problem and please help me because I don't know—"

"Whoa, whoa." Nash squeezed me tight and shushed me.

I breathed. Tears rolled down my cheeks. Nash's heartbeat thumped in my ear, soft and steady.

"It's okay. We're gonna be okay. Harper and Mendez are still groggy. Give 'em a minute, then we'll go find that sonofa…gun. We'll find him and he ain't gonna hurt nobody ever again. Okay?" Nash's drawl somehow made everything better.

His arms reminded me of sitting on Ethan's lap, watching rocket launches on TV. Those memories made me feel loved, wanted, and safe. I hadn't felt safe in forever. Since Ethan left.

His words, on the other hand, confused me. Until I realized he had no idea what I meant because he didn't know I'd heard him earlier. Duh. Use your brains, Emma.

Without letting go of me, Nash pointed to the screwdriver in Baldwin's hand. Thick, dark liquid stained the blade and Baldwin's hand. "Where'd you get that?"

I didn't want to think about the dark liquid or how it got there. "Found it. I hid from the alien guy in a bedroom, and it was in the closet with other broken stuff."

"Who leaves a screwdriver in a closet?"

Thinking of the small toolbox in my own closet, I blushed.

"Somebody who likes tools," Baldwin said.

Nash chuckled. "I guess I'm glad you found the closet of somebody like that, because it made a huge difference. What else did you do while we were separated?"

Ethan appeared in the doorway, leaning against the frame and holding his head. "Sitrep." He sounded like someone had hit him in the head with a brick.

After giving me one last squeeze, Nash let go. "Emma found us. Baldwin stabbed the alien guy in the hand with her screwdriver. I've got his zappy weapon thing. He ran off."

"I'll bet he's going to either the screens room or his ship." I wiped my face on my sleeve, grateful for once that I wore no makeup. "And he has my gun someplace."

"Screens room?" Ethan asked.

"Ship?" Baldwin asked at the same time.

Nash touched my shoulder. "The gun is bad news."

"Everything is this way." I pointed.

Ethan wobbled, trying to head in that direction. Mendez crawled through the doorway. We'd have to let the alien guy get away, I figured.

"Baldwin and I can scout it," Nash said. "You follow. Slow as you need."

"No. We're not splitting up with a verified hostile loose in the facility." Ethan shook his head and winced. "Maybe we should retreat for today."

Oops. I gulped. "We can't. The sentinels started targeting Akata, so she left. We have to stay at least until she comes back."

The guys glanced at each other. Any moment, they'd berate me for letting her leave, or not fleeing with her, or something.

Mendez shrugged. "Sounds like do or die."

"We maybe could hole up," Nash said, "but that ain't gonna get us anywhere except back in a box."

Ethan grumbled under his breath. "Fine. Mendez, get on your feet. Emma, explain and lead on."

We set a brisker pace than I expected. Mendez shambled, using the wall for support. Ethan seemed to grit his teeth and soldier through whatever pain he felt.

As we followed the trail to the stairs, I explained what had happened and what I'd found. I left out the part where I'd overheard Nash. The whole thing sounded much less scary as a quick story. By the time I reached the end of my stupid recounting, I expected the guys to laugh at me.

"Good work," Ethan said as we climbed down the stairs. He recovered faster than I had. He also sounded genuine, not sarcastic.

Baldwin nodded like he agreed.

Nash grinned. "You're a regular spitfire."

"I should've—"

"Nope," Mendez said. "No shouldas, wouldas, or couldas. You did what you were able at the time. We don't armchair quarterback here." He patted my shoulder.

I wanted to kiss him. Ethan acted like I expected. The rest of the guys didn't. Everyone I knew from high school would've teased or made a snide comment about something in my story. I could almost hear Andy asking why I didn't flash the alien. He and the other boys would've laughed and high-fived each other.

Mendez, Nash, and Baldwin listened, accepted, and praised. I felt like I'd proven myself as part of the team. They knew about my problem and they still wanted me.

They wanted me. Not my body, but me. Nobody wanted me except Ethan. Not even Mom and Dad wanted me. Madison wanted someone else to help deflect Andy and other boys. Bridget wanted... Thinking about it, I didn't know what

Bridget and Tiffany had ever gained from having me around. Did they even consider me their friend?

What did that word mean to Bridget? What did it mean to me? I considered Bridget and Tiffany my friends, but couldn't remember the last time either said something nice to me. I'd spent tons of time worrying about their reactions to me. They knew about my problem and made fun of it. Once, Bridget had threatened to tell the school nurse if I didn't drive her to a party.

She didn't care. She'd never cared. Neither had Tiffany. They both seemed like they wanted someone to pick on. In exchange, I got to experience guys like Andy and Tom. What a great fringe benefit. Not.

We reached the last corner before the hallway where the alien guy had docked his ship. Mendez pointed for me to stop and wait while the guys surrounded the passage.

Leaning against the wall, I watched them gesture to each other to communicate. Nash, still carrying the taser-thingy, ducked around the corner first. Baldwin brandished the screwdriver shank and followed. Ethan and Mendez had no weapons. They stormed the hallway anyway. Like Marines.

I heard boots clomping, then nothing. Mendez popped his head around the corner. "It's clear." He beckoned me closer.

When I stepped around the corner, I saw Ethan, Nash, and Baldwin checking the place where the alien's ship had docked. No light glowed. Some kind of door blocked the hole.

Alien guy had sealed the ship access without leaving.

"He might still be on the station, or he might be on the ship," Mendez said.

"I think I can get a few of the screens running again."

"I was hoping you'd say that." Mendez whistled to get everyone's attention.

The other guys turned to look. Mendez pointed at me and the living quarters hallway. We waited for them to join us, then I led them past the bedrooms.

Inside the screens room, I noticed the bottom plate

with the single screw hung at an angle. I should've used two. If I'd taken the time, though, the alien guy would've caught me.

Without waiting for someone to order me, I ducked behind the screens. If we wanted screens, I had to untangle the wires and put some back. The last few I'd done seemed plausible, at least.

"I think I can get two or three running in a few minutes. I need the screwdriver."

Baldwin handed it to me in silence.

He didn't check out my butt or glance at my chest. The entire exchange consisted of him presenting the screwdriver and me taking it.

When we got home, I wanted to stick with these guys. Until then, I wanted to ask them questions. I felt like they'd give me honest answers, even about weird or uncomfortable stuff, without balking or accusing me of anything.

I could see the four guys through a thin, horizontal slice of space between the individual screens. "Ethan?"

"Yeah?"

"Would you ever stick your hand up a girl's skirt?"

They all glanced at each other like this confirmed some theory.

Ethan's jaw clenched. "Only if she wanted me to."

Baldwin met my gaze with an intensity like he wanted to punch someone other than me. Ethan looked at the screens to the side. Mendez and Nash both crossed their arms and shifted to watch for the alien guy.

"How would you know that?"

"How would I know if a woman wanted me to touch her?" Ethan's nose flared. "I'd ask."

He'd ask. I frowned as I straightened a wire with my fingers. By the strictest definition, Andy had asked for what he wanted. Not really, though, and he was the only one.

"What if she didn't say no?"

Ethan crossed his arms. His fists clenched so hard his knuckles turned white. "Default is no. It's not yes unless it's a clear yes."

Baldwin dipped his head in a subtle, shallow nod of agreement.

I'd heard Nash say he'd noticed one more thing. Was I so easy to read? How did he even pick up on that? Mind-reading? Had Akata told him something after rifling through my head? No, that didn't sound right. She could, but I didn't think he'd ask.

"The screen is working," Ethan said.

Right. We had a job to do. Find the alien guy and subdue him, switch all the defenses offline, reprogram the wormhole device, and go home. None of those steps seemed doable.

"Does it show anything?" I shifted to the next screen.

"Empty hallway," Baldwin said.

I nodded. "There are motion sensors and cameras all over the station, so our alien guy is hiding."

"Nash, Mendez, sweep these rooms. Expect ambush."

The two men nodded and left the room.

Ethan glanced at me. "Baldwin, stand watch." His attention returned to the working screen.

Baldwin nodded and stepped outside the doorway.

The silence in the room reminded me of sitting at the dinner table, waiting for Dad to decide we could leave. Shared frustration bonded us.

I fixed the second screen and moved to a third.

Ethan watched them with his arms crossed. "I'm sorry I wasn't there to stop him."

"Who?"

"The boy who hurt you."

The screwdriver slipped. My hand whacked a screen on a sharp edge. It hurt. I hissed and checked it. Blood welled in a thin scrape across the skin between the forefinger and thumb.

"Are you okay?"

"It's nothing." I sucked on it because I didn't have any

real antiseptic options.

"Is that what you said after he hurt you?"

I choked. My cheeks burned and my eyes watered. Ethan appeared beside me. He wrapped his arms around me and held my head to his chest. Why couldn't I do anything for him except cry?

"I love you, Emma. You're important and have value. You're not worthless, you're not fat, and you're for damned sure not a freak. You don't have to do anything you don't want just because someone else wants it. Ever. You can say no. The things you've already done don't define you, they're just your past."

How did he know what to say? On the screen, he'd claimed he had no idea. "Help me," I whispered.

"I promise. We have to get out of this mess first, though. Do you think you can get a few more screens working?"

I mattered. I had value. I wasn't fat or a freak.

The ideas sounded hollow inside my head. I knew what I looked like. So did Ethan, of course, but he would never see me the same as anyone else. If I had a porcelain bowl handy, I knew I'd purge.

Stuck on a space station with an alien, in an unknown part of the universe nowhere near Earth, hoping to figure out a way home, and I wanted to barf. Pathetic.

Nodding and sniffling, I pulled away. One more screen, one more set of cameras, one more chance to find the alien.

Ethan kissed my forehead and returned to watching the screens.

I attacked the nearest screw.

CHAPTER 25

"That's all I can do," I told Ethan. Ten screens worked. The rest of the wires hung in a wild clump, too damaged by my earlier actions for a quick fix. Ethan hadn't spotted the alien in the time it had taken me to fix the screens. At a guess, I thought ten or fifteen minutes had passed.

Nash and Mendez stood at the doorway, keeping watch for the alien. They hadn't found anything in their sweep. Baldwin stared at the screens with Ethan.

I slipped around to stand at Ethan's side. The screens all showed blank, empty hallways.

"I guess he knows where the cameras are," I said. "Or he's inside his ship and hasn't left for some reason."

"Yeah," Ethan said. "What would I do in his situation? I'm alone on a mission and I found loose hostiles who managed to disarm me. They injured me without killing me. First priority is escape. Second is medical triage. Third is evaluating mission parameters, which we don't know."

"It's probably safe to assume his mission parameters include station security," Mendez said. "He's going to concern himself with personal safety first, though, then station security."

"We gotta expect him to call for reinforcements, even if he can't," Nash said.

I blinked. Reinforcements meant more guys with more

taser-thingies. They probably had bigger ones too. Like the big ones orbiting the station. "Why isn't he using the sentinels?"

"Good question." Ethan tapped one of the screens and squinted at the symbols on the menu. "Maybe he doesn't have access to the controls. If he does, maybe he doesn't want to accidentally target himself because he doesn't know where we are or what we're doing."

The idea of the second option made him seem less alien. He hadn't killed anyone, after all. If he believed we would hurt him when given a chance, his actions made sense. I wondered whether he looked at us like we looked at monkeys or tigers.

All my studying didn't help me with that problem.

"Harper, this station has living quarters for two dozen, and we've seen exactly one guy." Mendez glanced inside. I felt his eyes on me, but I didn't feel queasy. He didn't stare at my body. Instead, he looked at me like Ethan did. Like he saw a person. "Most of the facility is automated, but I bet it needs those two dozen people to run at peak efficiency, or else it wouldn't have those living quarters. So this guy is some kind of specialist, here to do one thing."

"We don't know what that one thing is, but it sure as heckfire ain't soldiering. He must've expected the facility to be safe."

I raised my brow at Nash. "He carried a weapon."

Nash raised the taser-thingy. "This thing? This ain't a weapon. This here is a personal self-defense doodad. Like having a can of pepper spray in your purse. Might even be some tool-like purpose for it in a place like this. I'd try figuring it out if I thought I could without accidentally tasing someone."

Though I instantly wanted to ask for the taser-thingy so I could try using it, I saw his point. We didn't know how it worked. Aiming the pointy end and pressing the button could cause it to affect anyone in the general vicinity of the target area. I doubted it. Like Nash, I still didn't want to risk it.

"The point is," Ethan said, "he's clearly not a soldier. More likely, he came to perform maintenance or repairs on something."

"Like the wormhole device?"

Everyone turned to stare at me. I blushed.

The guys all glanced at each other. Ethan nodded. "Let's check the wormhole room. That is, after all, our goal."

I wanted to protest. With time to review the menus and actions with Akata, I thought I could decipher some of the symbols. Having that knowledge seemed useful. More tools would make me feel more secure about trying to reverse the wormhole. The Akata suit would give me someone with expertise to ask questions.

Besides all that, I didn't want to go home. I did! But I totally didn't. Out here, I had this great group of guys ready to support me in anything. They trusted me and let me do what I could instead of berating me for what I couldn't. With them, I felt safer than when I locked myself in my bedroom.

At home, waiting for me, I had Bentley. If I decided to back out of Bentley, I had nothing. Dad wouldn't support me doing something else any more than he'd supported Ethan. My skills could get me a job working a cash register someplace. I'd never build rockets or spaceships.

Out here, no one cared about degrees or grades, they cared about results. With the right tools and materials, I could build whatever I wanted. No one would stop me for a lack of qualifications.

Wanting to stay made me feel selfish and horrible. Ethan probably wanted a girlfriend. The other guys had families, and also probably wanted to start their own. I had no right to stand in their way.

We didn't have Akata to fall back to, the alien guy would probably make sure we couldn't storm the facility again, and the guys wanted to go home.

I took a deep breath, squared my shoulders, and accepted reality. We needed to go home, and the guys needed me to make it happen. So I'd make it happen. Somehow.

Nash brandished the taser-thingy and led the group back up the stairs. He and Baldwin checked and cleared every corner and doorway we used. They followed the trail of black stuff until they recognized their surroundings, then turned and led us to the wormhole room.

Having seen it with Akata's help, I knew what to expect. It seemed so much bigger than it had when Akata showed me, though. The wide ramp to the platform with the mirror towered over me from across the room. White lights glared down from the high ceiling, throwing harsh shadows. A dozen inactive robots lined one wall.

The guys checked every nook and cranny for robots and aliens before letting me enter the room.

At that moment, it occurred to me that we were the aliens here. The blue-skinned man belonged. We didn't.

As soon as Ethan said I could, I hurried around the huge gun-shaped thing hanging from the ceiling to reach the control panel behind the glass wall. Like Akata had shown me, it had switches, knobs, buttons, and a large screen. I recognized the button that activated the wormhole devices.

While the guys kept watch, I tapped the screen. It flickered to life and showed a lot of options in button format with that same writing as the other screen menus. Hoping for a match, I scanned every listing. Several included pieces I recognized, but none had the same words.

I wanted to pry off the panels and examine the wiring underneath. Without knowing how it worked, I doubted I could do that and avoid damaging it. That left me with experimentation.

"Everyone stay away from the platform." No one had approached it, but better safe than sucked through to a different world.

My first button choice opened a new page with square. Each square held two things—a circle filled with colors and more writing. One stood out among them because I'd recognize a rendering of Earth anywhere. Even among other planets with similar blue and green coloration, nothing quite matched Italy's boot like Italy.

Aside from the geographic resemblance, it had an X in the box in the corner. Each of the other options had an empty box. Given it had been the last place the device connected to, it made sense for Earth to remain selected.

The screen showed eleven other worlds, and had an arrow that I thought indicated another page. These blue-skinned people had constructed a wormhole creating device and knew at least a dozen worlds with living creatures worth dragging across for their purposes.

Despite their technological prowess, they used knobs, switches, and buttons for this control panel, and treadmills for their clunky robots. Priorities, I guess.

Part of me wanted to know why they did it and what the lepiku had to do with it. The rest just wanted to get through this. With the language barrier, even if our alien guy knew the answer and wanted us to know, he couldn't tell us.

"Incoming!" Baldwin dove against the wall.

Thin arcs of blue-white energy flew through the door. They curved toward Baldwin but hit the wall beyond him. Nash pointed his taser-thingy and fired a return volley of electricity.

I shrank to the floor with a squeak. Panic cranked up my heartrate to infinity.

"Emma! Keep working! We've got you covered!"

Ethan's shout cut through everything. I trusted them to protect me. If anything happened to me, it would be because it also happened to them first. Covering my face, I tried to shut out the crackle and zap, the grunt and groan of a taser battle. The guys watched over me.

With a deep breath, I stood and turned. No matter what, I would keep my eyes on my task and ignore everything happening behind me.

I could do this.

CHAPTER 26

I had no idea how to do this. Four men's lives depended on me doing this.

When I tapped on the Earth box, it showed me a larger version of the box. Lines of symbols offered information I couldn't decipher. No help there. The arrow, at least, I understood. Back on the screen with the planets in boxes, I made sure Earth remained checked. Then I backed out of that menu and examined others.

Behind me, men grunted and groaned. Electricity crackled. Flares cast harsh, short-lived shadows across the screen. Metal crashed. Someone squealed.

Cringing against the noise and what I imagined happening on the other side of the glass wall, I kept tapping things. Each screen showed me something different that I didn't understand.

Until I stumbled across one that made complete sense.

It showed a sphere on one side and an ellipse on the other. Animated arrows pointed from the sphere to the ellipse, like a wind flow diagram. Getting the arrows to point the other way would reverse the direction of the wormhole.

Probably.

In theory.

As soon as I switched them, I could hit the button and we would go home. Ethan wanted that. Mendez, Baldwin, and

Nash wanted that. I could watch them go and not follow. Staying here meant no more Bentley, no more friends, and no more Ethan. I'd mourned Ethan, so maybe I could handle it.

Staying here also meant dealing with creatures I couldn't understand. By myself. The blue-skinned guy might even decide I couldn't do whatever job he wanted me for and throw me back home anyway.

Or kill me. He could kill me.

At least at home, I'd have Ethan to help me. We'd have other human beings. Maybe Ethan and I together could convince Dad to let me do what I wanted. And if not, we could find someplace else together.

I tapped and swiped every part of the screen until the arrows pointed the other way.

Turning to tell the guys, I saw Ethan drag the blue-skinned guy into the room by his neck and shove him to the floor, face-first. He held my little gun. In his hand, it seemed like a tiny toy. Nash held the taser-thingy pointed at the alien. Baldwin kicked him. Mendez entered the room holding a slim rifle and pointed it at the blue-skinned guy.

They'd disarmed him and all seemed fine.

"Emma?" Ethan called over his shoulder.

I hurried to the edge of the glass wall. "I think I figured it out."

"Are you willing to bet all our lives on it?" Mendez asked.

Glancing back at the screen and the wind diagram, I took a moment to consider the question. If I was wrong, we'd all die. If I was right, we'd all end up spat out of some mirror someplace, and that might also not turn out well.

If we all might die, I needed to say something first.

"Ethan?"

"Yeah, Cog?" He kept his eyes on the alien.

"I...I have..." The b word didn't want to come out of my mouth.

Ethan turned and saw me. "You have what? Doubts?"

160

I had a problem, and I had to say it out loud or nothing would change. If we all died, I wanted to go knowing I'd faced it, knowing it hadn't beaten me. If everything worked and the wormhole took us home, I needed help, and I couldn't say if I'd have the courage again anytime soon. Not if I also had to face everything else in my life.

"A problem. I have a problem. It's called b—bulimia."

I barely heard Nash murmur, "Attagirl."

Ethan smiled at me.

My eyes itched and watered. The corners of my mouth refused to stay still. I expected static but didn't get any.

"We'll beat it, Cog. I believe in you."

"I got your back too," Mendez said.

The alien guy surged to his feet. He leaped at Nash and swiped for the taser-thingy. Nash moved so fast I couldn't track what he did. Bodies blurred with motion. The alien guy stumbled toward the door. Mendez smacked him with the butt of his new rifle. Baldwin slid into the fray and swept the alien's leg.

Ethan strolled to my side like nothing happened behind him. He trusted the other guys so much more than I'd ever trusted anyone in my whole life. Except Ethan. My rock stood and offered me a safe haven in the midst of chaos.

Baldwin followed the alien out with his fist, holding the screwdriver on its way to the alien's face. Mendez slipped out to back him up.

I didn't want to know what happened in the hallway. Ethan wrapped his arms around me and squeezed. Nothing else mattered.

"When we get home, I'm going to tell Dad that you're not going to Bentley. And if he disagrees, then we'll tell him to go to hell and figure something else out." His voice rumbled in his chest and warmed my heart.

Remembering the red sticks in my pocket, I pulled one out and showed him. "These might be worth something on Earth, just like they are out here."

"They might, yeah. Good work, Cog. You've saved the day, armed with space coral, a screwdriver, and your brain. That's pretty impressive."

I grinned. "I think your muscles helped? A little?"

He laughed.

"Hostile neutralized," Mendez said. "Can we go home now?"

Ethan and I turned to see the three guys. Baldwin shut the door.

"Emma?" Ethan pulled away far enough to see his face. "Are you ready?"

Nodding, I let go. "We should maybe all stand behind the glass wall when I start it up, in case anything goes wrong."

The five of us huddled behind the wall. Everyone watched while I pushed the button. As in Nash's memory, The gun-like part whirred and spun. The thick barrel pulled back to expose a coil suspended between two prongs.

Instead of white light, the tip blasted the mirror with black so dark it absorbed the light in the room. Pressure beat against my ears. I covered them with my hands. The silvery surface rippled. Darkness formed a sphere in the center with thin tendrils writhing across the surface. The gun cracked loud enough to make me jump, firing a bolt of magenta.

With that, I got the hint. In the memory Akata had shown me, the bolts fired white, yellow, blue-green, reddish purple, then black. Reversing the direction of the wormhole meant reversing the order of the bolts.

Someday, I'd work with the idea of colored light, force, and mirrors to create a similar technology for humans. Crossing the distance from Earth to Mars in a second could change so many things for us. Physics would have to race to keep up with my research.

The blue-green bolt fired, adding its color to the dark magenta swirl. Yellow, then white fired, to engulf the rest. To my surprise, the final blast made everything white, as with before. It covered the entire mirror and pulsed with weaving tendrils flashing across the room. We all remained unaffected behind the glass wall.

"Is anyone else having second thoughts?" Mendez asked.

Baldwin and Nash both murmured their agreement.

Ethan grinned. "It looks scary, but we've faced worse things than death."

"Like Kidd's idea of cooking," Nash said.

The guys chuckled. I didn't say anything. If they wanted to stay, then I would too. And I wanted that, but I didn't want to wheedle or force them. Whatever we did, we'd do it together.

Nash sobered first. "We're gonna have to explain what happened to the rest of the guys."

"Akata has all their dogtags," Mendez said. "We should've thought to bring them."

"No shoulda, woulda, coulda," I chided.

Mendez grinned.

Ethan laid his hand on my shoulder. "Our friend with the blue skin probably called for reinforcements, so we need to do this now or never. "

"Home," Baldwin said. "It's home."

That word meant something to me, but I had a feeling it wasn't the same thing as Baldwin. To me, it meant comfort and safety. It meant people I could trust and count on.

In short, I was already home. The rest? Just geography.

OTHER BOOKS BY THE AUTHOR

Spirit Knights
young adult urban fantasy
Girls Can't Be Knights
Backyard Dragons
Ethereal Entanglements
Ghost Is the New Normal
Boys Can't Be Witches
War of the Rose Covens (coming May 2019)

Maze Beset trilogy
superhero science fiction
Dragons In Pieces
Dragons In Chains
Dragons In Flight
Superheroes in Denim (compilation)

Fantasy in the Ilauris setting
sword and sorcery fantasy
Damsel In Distress
Shadow & Spice (short story)
Al-Kabar

WWW.AUTHORLEEFRENCH.COM

The Greatest Sin
(with Erik Kort)

epic fantasy

The Fallen
Harbinger
Moon Shades
Illusive Echoes
A Curse of Memories

Darkside Seattle

cyberpunk

Street Doc
Fixer
Mechanic
Hacker
Meat (coming 2019)

Anthology Appearances

Into the Woods: a fantasy anthology
Merely This and Nothing More: Poe Goes Punk
Unnatural Dragons: a science fiction anthology
What We've Unlearned: English Class Goes Punk
Hideous Progeny: Horror Goes Punk
Bridges (as editor)
Carnival (as editor)
Swords, Sorcery, & Self-Rescuing Damsels (coming April 2019)

ABOUT THE AUTHOR

Lee French lives in Olympia, WA, with two kids, two bicycles, and too much stuff. She is an avid gamer and a member of the Myth-Weavers online RPG community. In addition to spending too much time there, she also trains in taekwando, keeps a nice flower garden with one dragon and absolutely no lawn gnomes, works an excessive number of book events, and tries in vain every year to grow vegetables that don't get devoured by neighborhood wildlife.

She is an active member of the Science Fiction and Fantasy Writers of America and the Northwest Independent Writers Association, as well as serving the Olympia region as a NaNoWriMo Municipal Liaison.

If you enjoyed this book, please take a moment to review it wherever you purchase your books or ebooks.